CHOOSING BRAVERY

LONESOME HEARTS SERIES

JACQUI NELSON

Cover design by The Killion Group, Inc
ISBN ebook: 978-0-9936387-9-4
ISBN print: 978-0-9936387-8-7

DEDICATION

For all the readers who enjoy a book and then write a book review.

Writing is, more often than not, a solitary battle. Your kind words make us brave enough to keep going.

PRAISE FOR THE LONESOME HEARTS SERIES...

Between Heaven & Hell

"A perfect, steady-paced book with poetic descriptions of romance and easy-to-follow fluidity of Callahan and Hannah's journeys." ~ Chanticleer Book Reviews

"A fire-cracker of a love story with the perfect blend of fascinating characters, intense emotion, historical drama and fast-paced action." ~ Scarlett Penn

"Beautiful writing and flawed characters it was easy to care about. A thoroughly engaging story I enjoyed tremendously." ~ Lark

"An exciting journey filled with perilous adventure, this is an original interesting tale with a woven plot line that comes full circle." ~ InD'tale Magazine

Following Faith

"The first story I'd read by Jacqui Nelson which put her on my watch-out-for-and-read-her-stuff list. Despite the short length, this story packed a big punch." ~ Michelle R.

"So well written and so descriptive, you easily get transported to the old west and are traveling on the trail with Faith and Eagle. A beautiful, sweet, romantic, heartwarming story you won't want to miss." ~ Barb

Jacqui Nelson "has a unique way of drawing the reader back to the old west with colorful descriptions and characters who leap from the page." ~ Jacquie B.

Choosing Bravery

"Grand adventure. Mystery and excitement." ~ Sandra S.

"Action packed, fabulous setting and two main characters you could really root for" ~ N. Love

"One of those stories that just takes you away to a world of the wild west, filled with adventure, suspense and sweet romance. I couldn't put it down." ~ B

Rescuing Raven - free for my newsletter subscribers

"Grabbed my interest from the first page and did not let go until the end." ~ Babs

CHAPTER 1

Cascade Mountains, Oregon – 1868

The scent of fresh blood on an undercurrent of primeval decay choked Élodie Rousseau, nearly bringing her to her knees. She strove to keep her steps silent in the snow below the cave's gaping black maw. High above the evergreens stretching to the mountain peak, the midday sun blazed down. The pocket of white shone brutally bright but gave no warmth.

A cold sweat chilled her to the bone and played havoc with her grip on her rifle. The scream that sent her sprinting up the final leg of the ascent still rang in her ears, echoing with disbelief and horror.

Gray Owl was right. Only death lived in this once sacred place.

A wise daughter of the land would've heeded her

old friend's warning to stay away, to look to the future, to focus on her gift of helping people find their way in the wilderness... rather than getting lost in the past. But death was what had drawn her to this isolated mountain cave.

Were her parents inside? After sixteen years, would she finally find their remains only to stay with them forever?

The leather-skinned prospector she'd heard drowning his demons in Fort Shelton's rum-hole had babbled like a spooked greenhorn. This cavern, he'd proclaimed, contained far too many bones. The human kind. Lost loved ones lay here. Long forgotten.

Not so her parents. She'd never stopped searching for a glimpse of them in everyone she met.

Behind a jagged fall of rock, barely a dozen strides up the slope, the humped shoulders of a giant creature rose like a phantom.

She froze with her finger on her rifle's trigger. Her adoptive father, Eagle Feather's advice steadied her hand: *Never shoot until you see, with clear eyes, what you might kill.*

With an echoing snort, the creature disappeared into the cave. The tips of its dark fur flashed like frosted silver with the sudden movement. The fear threatening to suffocate her vanished as well. She hadn't stumbled upon an evil spirit, but a grizzly bear guarding its den and maybe its cubs.

The smell of a battle—blood and gore but no gunpowder—remained strong. It came from a wall of dark green firs on her left. Glancing between the trees and the black hole, she hastened toward the bear's prey. The snow plummeted into a ravine. A slash of scarlet severed the white in two.

Down to the bottom and up the other side, someone had rolled, then crawled. Eluding the bear and saving their life. Temporarily. With that much blood lost, they wouldn't last long.

She cast a final look at the cave.

Nothing stirred. At least as far as she could see.

She sprinted down the gulch. The frigid air bit her lungs, puffed out in wraithlike bursts. In the middle, the thigh-deep snow weighed on her legs like chains. She fell, struggled to her feet, slogged across, and up the other side. Her feet found solid ground. She marshaled her strength for the final push.

She vaulted over a fallen tree, landed in a crouch, and froze—face-to-face with a man slumped against the stump.

Wide and wild, the man's dark pupils nearly obliterated his pale blue irises. He stared at her through a waterfall of blood spilling from too-many-to-count slashes across his dark hair and ashen face, but somehow miraculously missing his eyes. He didn't blink.

Dread constricted her chest and trapped her breath. Was he dead? Had she reached him too late?

She searched for a sign of life in his broad frame. He clutched a long-barreled Winchester 66—a rifle coveted for its accuracy and firepower by both big game and bounty hunters—against a jacket shredded with more bloody claw marks.

She leaned closer to him.

A low growl rumbled in his throat. Or was it a groan? Whatever it was, the sound proved he still lived. His wounds would become scars mightier than Gray Owl's or Eagle Feather's or anyone's she'd ever seen—if she could keep him alive.

Looping the strap of her old carbine rifle over her shoulder, she reached out to him with both hands. "I need to stop your bleeding."

He dove sideways and scrambled away on his elbows and belly. One of his legs trailed behind him. Twisted at an unnatural angle. Limp and broken.

"Stop!" She struggled to keep her voice low as she attempted to grab hold of him. "You're making your injuries worse."

He evaded her. Even ripped apart, he was a wily opponent. But she wasn't his adversary.

"*Nom de Dieu,*" she grumbled. "Quit being ornery." She lunged and snared the tail of his jacket.

He collapsed on his side.

"I only want to—"

The muzzle of his rifle striking her chest halted

her words. Beneath the hard press of iron, her heart missed a beat, then took off at a gallop.

She slowly raised her palms. "Don't shoot. I mean you no harm."

His gaze darted over her and the forest around them with a feverish intensity, but his rifle didn't budge. She pushed back the fur-lined hood of her coat so he could see her better. He closed his eyes and shook his head, as if rejecting a dreadful sight.

She strained to hear in the silence that followed. No bear or creature of any sort approached. Or so she hoped.

"You're safe with me." She repeated her words in French and then the Spanish she'd learned from her uncle Alejandro. She even tried the local dialect of the Molalla that Gray Owl had taught her. When the stranger showed no reaction of understanding any of those languages, she switched back to English.

"Trust me," she urged. "Open your eyes. I'm not your enemy."

A tortured grimace sealed his eyes even tighter.

"We don't have time for this." She tamped down the impatience hardening her voice and strove for a sweeter tone. "I can help you. Ask any of the locals. They'll tell you I'm a first-rate guide, a steadfast friend." She stifled her sigh.

They'd also say she was dangerously impulsive, to herself and to him. If she hadn't charged blindly to the rescue, she wouldn't be wasting precious seconds scrambling to gain his trust before he died.

The pressure of his rifle against her eased. His strength was fading.

Her mind sped through the steps to save him: stitch his wounds, splint his leg, and drag him down the mountain to the nearest settlement.

On the long trail westward, Auntie Hannah had saved Uncle Paden's life using a travois. This man shared Paden's sturdy size. A small concern. Hannah had shown that a man's weight was no match for a woman's determination.

The snow would help. She could build a sled from fir branches and cheat the reaper as well—if this man let her.

"Lay down your weapon and we can help each other. Together we're stronger."

"Lies. All lies!" His words exploded with surprising strength.

The click of his rifle being cocked said the rest. Disbelief shook her like a deer realizing too late she'd run up against a wolf. She'd die here after all.

Would she find her parents in the land beyond? Before she embraced that final journey, she yearned to explore so much more on Earth. The world was a bigger place than the home she cherished, a home that had given her strength but limited her growth. This man and his rifle were proof of that.

She wanted to learn, to live, to fall in love. All she

had to do was end the life of a man who, judging by his wounds, would surely die today anyway.

"Kill me," he whispered.

Shock made her flinch. Had he heard her thoughts? Why had he come to her mountain? What demons did he shut his eyes against and wrestle inside his head? Would anyone miss him if she put her future above his?

"Kill me. Or...I'll kill you." His halting words pierced her heart like arrows. "Only...two choices. It's...what...you taught me."

She stiffened with outrage. Who'd taught him that?

"You decide," he urged. "Don't wait. Choose." He'd placed his life in her hands.

She easily found her rifle but struggled to raise it against him.

Instead, her gaze lifted to the bright sunlight dancing above the dark evergreens. Her voice was hoarse but determined when she spoke. "I've been taught differently. Never shoot until you see, with clear eyes, what you might kill. I choose bravery."

CHAPTER 2

Four months later...

Through the trees circling the cave where his humanity had almost ended, Lachlan Bravery saw everything his heart desired and dreaded. His wildly beautiful savior had finally left him. Élodie Rousseau had taken her sharp wit and tender heart and returned to the place that had torn him apart.

After a grim childhood in the far north and an equally arduous rise to fame crisscrossing the continent hunting fugitives, how could such a small patch of earth—that he'd only seen once and now couldn't remember clearly—have this much power over him? He'd survived too much for his strength to desert him completely.

Ignoring the aches and pains nagging his still mending flesh, weakened by months of lying flat on his back, he limped to the edge of the trees separating him from Élodie and the cave, and froze.

The familiar nightmare roared down the mountain and hit him like a landslide.

Lashes of freezing cold and scorching heat bit his flesh. The seasons—then years—whipped by, blinding him. As did his struggles to find the outlaw gang who'd murdered his mentor.

Crazed laughter rang in his ears as he caught each fugitive. Next came the condemnations, his and theirs, as he hauled them to jail. How could a famous tracker find them but not Jellon Jerome's body?

A monster's consumed your master. The beast's holed up in a cave.

An unearthly scream. Kill or be killed.

I choose bravery.

Three whispered words. They yanked him free from hell. Same as when he'd first heard them.

He came back to Earth with only Élodie Rousseau between him and absolute madness. His name on her lips had stopped him from putting a bullet in her heart. She hadn't been talking about choosing him, though. Back then she hadn't known his name or his reputation.

He ran a shaky hand through his hair and across his face, tracing the scars, reminding himself of what was real. His world was ugly and brutal, inside and out.

He had no bravery. No choices.

Save one.

Staying sane enough to keep Élodie away from this cavern and his insanity was all that mattered. He pushed past his weaknesses, out of the trees, and up the slope to halt her and Alexandre Duval. The man she'd left him for.

Surprise widened the Frenchman's dark eyes—so very different from the man's crown of golden hair. A glower of disapproval quickly followed. The leather-bound journal he'd been scribbling in shut with a gunshot sharp crack. After only a week at Fort Shelton, a fort in name but not in form, Duval had made it clear he disliked Lachlan intruding on what he'd decided was his territory: Élodie plus any artifacts or unusual land formations on this mountain.

Duval's gaze went to the cave first and Élodie second. He had his priorities wrong. When his focus finally found Lachlan again, the furrow on his brow deepened—a single wrinkle marring the man's perfect appearance and life.

Golden Boy huffed out a breath. "Why are you here, Tracker?" His river smooth voice couldn't be more different from Lachlan's backwoods rasp. The man's superiority rang clearest in his word choice. He'd yet to address Lachlan by his name. He'd chosen to reduce him to a single word.

Lachlan sealed his lips against firing back with the double-barreled moniker he'd given Duval. Verbal battles had never been his calling. No matter what he said, this suave Golden Boy would win.

Besides, a long time ago in another life, his profession and perfect track record had meant everything to him. Then Jellon had died. And every day he failed to find his mentor's body, the label of Tracker had chipped away at his self-worth until he despised the word.

But not today. Today, being a tracker had allowed him to find Élodie and stop her.

Her hazel eyes, usually sparking with so many emotions they rivaled an autumn forest at full blaze, shone with only one sentiment.

Concern.

She'd been aware of him lurking in the trees. She'd let him take his time choosing to turn back or join her and halt her ascent. He'd wasted too much time. She'd gotten too close to the cave. She stood two strides above him, one above Duval, with her back to—

His mind grappled for the words to explain the horror that had shredded his reality. If the devil's spawn sprang out of this rift, Élodie wouldn't see the monstrosity until it was too late. The woman he'd learned so much about during the months of his recovery was often impulsive but never flat-out careless.

Worry and bewilderment loosened his lips. His words burst out gruff and a hundred times more imprudent than she could ever be. "Why do you continue to put your life in jeopardy? You know you're not safe here."

Not with Duval and certainly not with me. Neither one of us can protect you.

A melancholy smile curved her lips. "You're right. This place hasn't changed, nor has my first reason for coming here."

"He is not right." Duval's fingers fidgeted with the top button on his fancy frock coat. "Nor is he welcome here."

"Oh, but he is. Lachlan is familiar with danger. And he and I both know that no one is safe." Despite her words, her stance remained relaxed. Her rifle rested in the cradle of her arm, on a bed of rose-colored velvet.

He'd watched a trapper, sporting a temper and a beard worthy of a billy goat, go down on both knees and present the tailored jacket to her like she was the Queen of England. In repayment, the cantankerous old-timer had declared, for Yellow Feather helping him.

Yellow Feather. On his final crusade south along the Cascades, he'd heard increasing talk of the guide's accomplishments. She'd risen in his mind to the stature of a mythical Amazon warrior. He'd never dreamed she'd add saving his life to her accolades or that she'd be so pretty—and unnervingly impulsive as well.

Her current stillness doubled his disorientation. One hand cupped the stock of her carbine, while the other fidgeted with a loose string on her embroidered sleeve. Then swiftly, but not fast enough to draw attention if a person wasn't watching, her hand moved.

Her thumb halted on her rifle's hammer, her forefinger on the trigger.

No fear rose inside him, only a healthy rush of alertness. Her vow steadied his mind. *You're safe with me. I'm not your enemy.*

He couldn't read her expression, but he could follow her gaze—straight to Duval.

Golden Boy had unbuttoned his coat. With his journal now stuffed in a pocket, his fingers were free to tap a pearl-handled revolver holstered on his hip. Duval's dandy gunfighter image was ruined by the pack on his back, festooned with two lanterns, one pickaxe, and many coils of rope. "You should have stayed in Shelton."

As should have Duval. A week ago, the Frenchman had boasted to anyone who'd listen that he'd come to Shelton to prepare the settlement for the arrival of his elite team, funded by a Parisian scientific society.

This morning, Élodie hadn't arrived for her daily visit or told Lachlan she'd be busy elsewhere. He'd gone hunting for her. Shelton's trappers and traders had revealed that Duval's party had sent word they'd arrive tomorrow. And Duval had hired Élodie to guide him to the cave today.

Rumors abounded that certain caverns in the area were geological wonders.

He didn't give an owl's hoot how wonderful they were. He only cared about the dangers inside that could leap outside and hurt Élodie. While Duval suddenly appeared hell-bent on claiming his grand discovery before anyone else, including his team.

"*Va-t'en!*" Duval ordered with a flick of his hand. "Go away. You are not needed. You resemble a walking corpse."

"He does not! I won't let him die. I need—" Élodie sucked in a sharp breath before continuing through gritted teeth. "The world needs him. But his decision to leave—or stay—is his. Not yours or mine."

Duval cleared his throat roughly. A dry sound like corn husks rustling in a rising wind, similar to the tone the Frenchman reserved for discussing him. "You, Mademoiselle, are too young to understand what the world needs, and too trusting."

Lachlan agreed. Not that Élodie was too young, but that she shouldn't trust Duval. Why had she chosen to come here with this egotistical jackass?

The simplest of answers made his gut twist. Duval had asked for her help, and Lachlan had not.

He'd been too busy vowing he'd never return and couldn't say why.

Élodie's chin rose to a resolute angle. "I may know nothing beyond these mountains, but I know Lachlan. He's held my future in his hands. He did not disappoint me that first day."

And all the days after? Lachlan's insides clenched even harder. He'd failed her as surely as he had Jellon.

Duval let his coat drop over his revolver and jabbed his finger at Lachlan. "*Regardez l'homme*. Look closely, Mademoiselle. Can you not see his skin is gray as ash? That he could keel over at any moment? He is a liability. For his own good and yours, he should go back."

"We should all go back," Lachlan muttered.

Élodie's gaze rose to the heavens, either seeking patience or a sign from a higher force. She had to be fed up with both Duval and him behaving like jackasses.

He wished for the hundredth time that the quagmire inside his head hadn't grown so deep. He didn't think he'd uttered a sound, but Élodie's eyes suddenly met his.

Her voice was firm when she spoke. "Sometimes we need to go back to go forward."

The steel in her voice steadied him, but her words did not.

She wasn't talking about him returning to Fort

Shelton, but both of them revisiting a place that haunted them equally. She'd waited as long as she could. Then Duval had asked her to guide him here. She probably viewed that as a message from the divine, a whisper from her spirit world.

Her resigned sigh ruffled his conscience and the quiet surrounding them. Unnaturally quiet. His gaze shot to the cave. The impenetrable blackness remained unchanged.

"Perhaps a compromise is best for everyone," she said. "Lachlan can wait here while Monsieur Duval and I go inside."

"That's only best for Golden Boy." Lachlan bit back his groan. He was now fully immersed in a battle he couldn't win or, most likely, even survive. The best he could do was to make sure Élodie lived. He straightened his back. "We are stronger together. I'm going with you."

A clatter of stones tumbled down the slope, coming from behind her.

He yanked his Winchester up to his shoulder and sighted down the barrel. Why he didn't know. His rifle hadn't helped him the last time he'd come here. With Élodie, his inability to pull the trigger had been a blessing. With the beast, it'd been an indefensible weakness—and not his first.

Another failure tormented him. This one from six years ago in a colony to the north under British rule and—for a time—a French menace.

A barrage of reprimands ricocheted in his skull, flaring bright and blinding.

Spineless. Ungrateful. Halfwit traitor! With each rebuke, Jellon struck him for letting him down and not finding him.

The ghostly arc of his arm rose above Lachlan, ready to deliver the death blow. A six-foot-tall wall of claws loomed over him, dripping blood.

Jellon's severed hand lay in a mining shaft hundreds of miles away.

"Don't shoot." Élodie's words cut him the deepest.

Was he aiming his Winchester at her again? The possibility wrenched him back to the here and now, and another hell.

Both he and Duval pointed their weapons in Élodie's direction.

He jumped in front of Duval. Mid leap, he snared the Frenchman's wrist and shoved his revolver skyward.

"Unhand me at once." Duval's glare cut from him to Élodie, now standing somewhere behind him. "The savage should have announced his presence."

"What're you talking about?" Lachlan demanded.

"The man lurking by the cave. His sudden

appearance had me thinking he was the bear they say bested you."

An avalanche of dread obliterated his ability to say another word. It did nothing to stifle his racing thoughts. Had his demon taken on a different skin? Why hadn't he returned and confronted the ungodly thing? Faced it alone, as he'd always done before meeting Élodie?

Because he didn't want to see whatever had attacked him. Not fully. He wouldn't allow Élodie to pay the price for his powerlessness to act.

He spun around, prepared to launch himself between her and whatever stood behind her.

Élodie's raised palm halted him. She'd remained in the same spot with her back to the mountain. Her rifle still rested in the crook of her arm. "Grizzlies do not usually choose to den in the same place twice."

"They embrace the wisdom of traveling to new ground." The comment came from Duval's savage—a silver-haired, bronzed-skinned man leaning against the rock to the right of the cave.

How had he not seen him before?

The newcomer's advice didn't stop Élodie from resuming her climb. As soon as she reached the man, she kissed both of his cheeks, pockmarked by illness, scarred by strife, and wrinkled by the passage of time. She performed the greeting in the graceful way of the French, but also with the solemn reverence of a devoted granddaughter.

"More delays," Duval grumbled as he elbowed Lachlan aside and followed in Élodie's footsteps.

Lachlan trailed a pace behind, striving not to favor his sore leg and draw attention. He kept his own gaze pinned on Duval until the man returned his revolver to its holster.

With barely a glance, Duval sidestepped Élodie and her friend and went straight to the entrance. He halted short of the darkness and craned his neck to peer inside as he doffed his pack and knelt to untie the lanterns.

When Lachlan reached the outcrop that protruded like a petulant lip from the mouth of the cavern, he planted himself beside Élodie, between her and Duval, and the gaping void. "Have you come to warn her against entering again?" he asked the old man.

He'd never met him, but based on his age and appearance, he had to be Gray Owl. During the long days of Lachlan's pain-filled recovery, Élodie had tried to distract him by telling him about the many people who'd shaped her life. When she was six, the Molalla chief had given her a sacred Medicine Hat horse and safe passage over his people's lands.

Gray Owl shook his head. "My counsel has been given and heard. I come to speak of other matters." He scanned Duval from head to foot, shook his head again, and faced Lachlan. "It lightens my heart to see my old friend has at least one new friend by her side. It makes it easier to say goodbye to my Ello."

The man's English was impressive. He'd had a devoted teacher. Élodie always gave as much as, or more than, she received.

She bowed her head, but not before he glimpsed the tears shining in her eyes. "I'll miss you, Grandfather."

"As will I." The old man laid his palm on her forehead and bowed his head as well. "May the Great Spirit guide your head today and your feet tomorrow as you journey to meet the rising sun."

Shock rendered Lachlan's voice little better than a croak. "You're leaving your mountains?"

Her gaze remained downcast. "This is my final day."

No! The word surged to his lips, then plummeted deep, like a dagger to his soul. She'd made her decision. And he faced his—one last day with her, in the worst of places.

A handful of strides away, Duval still knelt before the darkness. He held a slender, rectangular-shaped bundle wrapped in canvas. When he noticed Lachlan watching him, he shoved the bundle back inside his pack and busied himself lighting the lanterns waiting on the ground.

"You'll replace Duval's team," Lachlan said.

"He wishes to deliver his findings directly to his

society. We'll go as soon as his team arrives and he tells them what he's found."

"My time to depart has arrived as well." Gray Owl straightened his ancient frame. The conviction of a leader blazed in his eyes. "Always remember, my Ello, I will be with you. As will our mountains and our ancestors. We are one. We reside here." He tapped her heart.

Élodie flung her arms around the old man's neck. When she released him, they both wiped tears from their cheeks. With a quick nod and a surprisingly spry step for his age, Gray Owl descended the rocky slope and disappeared into the trees.

Élodie did not watch him go. As soon as the old man began his descent, she faced the cave. Gray Owl had been the reason she'd felt safe enough to keep her back to it previously, but not now.

"Gray Owl speaks true," he reassured her. "You are not alone."

"Neither are you, Lachlan." With each word, her voice became more hushed. "Tell me what torments you."

He pitched his voice low as well. "Why are you leaving? What's changed? You used to tell me everything."

"While you continue to say so little. You have many questions but give no answers to mine."

What could he tell her? That Duval was right?

That he was a walking corpse? That his body was mending, but his mind was damaged beyond repair?

"Speak now," she urged. "Before it's too late. What brought you to my mountain? What did you see here?"

"A ghost." His mouth went dry as dust. He swallowed hard. "From my past."

Her eyes widened in surprise but narrowed when he said no more. "A past you won't share with me?"

His throat seized tight. One word burst out. "Can't."

"Then the most I'll have is snippets of travelers' gossip about the legendary Lachlan Bravery, while you know nearly everything about me. You didn't have to ask who Gray Owl was. You knew because I've shared my entire past with you. I've never done that with anyone else." The quaver of hurt in her voice cut him to the core. "So be it. You've made your choice. You won't share any part of your life with me. But I choose differently."

"I wish—" *That I could be different.*

She leaned closer to him. "Do you still wish to learn what made me finally decide to leave my home?"

He nodded.

She rose on her toes. He leaned down to meet her halfway. Her hand found his and drew him closer. The stranglehold on his throat vanished. Air rushed into his lungs. How could he go on without her?

Her breath warmed his ear. "I'm leaving because I'm in love with you."

Astonishment rendered him mute.

"Now you know *everything* about me." She released him and dropped back on her heels.

The loss of her touch made the mountain lurch. The air chilled. The trees below and the rock above spun faster and faster, vanishing in a ghostly blur.

"You cannot feel this way. Not when I'm—"

"Do *not* tell me what I can and cannot do!"

The white nothing disappeared. Élodie filled his vision again.

Her eyes flashed and color rose high on her cheeks. "My feelings are mine. I make my own decisions. Today I choose to live, to learn, to secure my future far away from you. Who knows, maybe I'll find a new love in France."

CHAPTER 3

Quel *désastre!* Élodie's heart ached with regret. Lachlan stared at her like she'd shattered his world. Would she ever learn to consider the consequences before she plunged forward?

"You will love Paris." Alexandre Duval's confident reply made her shoulders slump.

Her disaster grew. How much had he heard?

Would her decision to start a new life be forever clouded by her old one? Alexandre already believed her too young and trusting. Did he now know she loved unwisely?

"No finer place exists." Crouched before the cave, Alexandre's attention remained on its murky interior, searching for his own way forward.

Maybe he'd only caught part of her declaration. One could hope.

Lachlan's eyes stayed on her, wide and wild and unreadable. Alarmingly similar to when they'd first met. Then time had healed him enough for glimpses of compassion and clarity. He'd seen beyond his own suffering. Until one day, she'd noticed him studying her with a riveting intensity.

No one had ever looked at her like that, like she was his entire reason for being. One couldn't build a future on the look in a man's eyes. Words, or lack of them, were important as well.

So were actions.

Her palm still tingled from touching him, wanting to reach out to him again. She'd been doing that every day for the last four months. Meanwhile, he'd maintained a determined distance. Close, but also far away.

You've made your choice. Get on with it.

"Wherever you go, Lachlan, I wish you well. I also bid you farewell." Careful not to brush up against him, she crossed the final steps. With her back to the man she loved, she took her place beside the man who'd used a plethora of words to entice her to join his adventures.

Alexandre's English was as gracefully accented as his French. His tongue smoothed the edges of some words and sharpened others. Every sentence came out refined but also effortless. She preferred the husky timbre of Lachlan's unvarnished voice, but like a starving stray, she'd gobbled up Alexandre's

tales of flamboyant feats and recitations of dry facts
with equal vigor.

Unlike Lachlan, the Frenchman did not guard
his words. He used them to shine a light on the
mysteries beyond her mountains.

"From this moment forward, everything shall be
different. Dedicate your heart and soul to my quest,
Mademoiselle, and we shall be well-rewarded."
Alexandre grasped a lantern in each hand. Without
them strapped to his pack, he rose to his feet with a
lot less noise.

He'd come well-prepared and had insisted on
carrying everything—until now. He handed one of
the lights to her. "The world is ours for the taking."

She appreciated his industrious energy and willingness to converse, but his disregard for others and
his eagerness to reach for his revolver disturbed her.

Lachlan may have pointed his Winchester her
way twice, but she'd never witnessed him raise a
finger toward anyone else. Today he hadn't even
blinked when Alexandre made a big show of threatening to use his revolver to make him leave.

Why did the manner in which a weapon was
drawn matter so much to her?

She certainly had a lot to learn. "I relish the
opportunity to explore unfamiliar lands and gain
wisdom from new acquaintances. Is your home in
Paris, Monsieur Duval?"

"Soon it will be." Despite his confident tone, he

didn't appear happy. Nor had his gaze left the cave. "We shall both thrive in Paris' culture and prestige. We will dress in the latest fashion, dine extravagantly, and be treated like royalty."

No mention of people. Had he lost someone dear to him as well?

"Do you have family there?" she asked.

"No." Alexandre's eyes narrowed. "They live in the country. Their moldering ancestral estate is only big enough to hold my father and his first-born son."

She waited for him to say more. He didn't, but at least he'd answered her question. So why did she feel like he was hiding as much as Lachlan?

She fought the compulsion to turn and see if the legendary fugitive hunter had accepted her goodbye and left. Her eyes stung as her regret rose again and blinded her. Looking back would do nothing but release a river.

Face forward. Put the past behind you.

"Shelton's residents told me about your parents." Alexandre patted her hand. "My condolences on your loss."

She blinked in surprise. He'd paused to share a simple kindness. A first.

"Thank you for your words, Monsieur Duval. They mean a great deal to me."

His gaze finally met hers, and he smiled. "Your voice is unusual, Mademoiselle. I recognize a hint of my homeland, but also the twang of Texas, the lilt of

Mexico, and several other unfamiliar but still distinct accents. Your cadence changes with each sentence, possibly each word. You are an intriguing conundrum and an exotic delight for my ears." When he paused, his brows rose expectantly. "I am eager to hear how your voice will describe mine."

"You are a silver-tongued flatterer, Monsieur, and not the first I've met. However, I find your voice interesting as well."

Alexandre's amusement flashed in a wide grin. "Now you flatter me."

Her own smile eased the tension gripping her. Maybe she could find a future with him. Her heart twisted painfully. Alexandre would never be Lachlan.

"You shall be my shining jewel. I will procure your stage and give you the world."

She stifled her sigh. One unadorned promise of shared adventures would've persuaded her swifter than this deluge of posturing.

Alexandre nodded with conviction. "Our similarities have already shaped the foundation for a perfect partnership. My family is lost to me as well."

The hitch in his voice when he spoke of family snared her attention and her compassion. "They need not stay that way. Reach out to them."

"Even if they stood a foot away, I could not reach them." His adamant tone made her frown.

"When did you last try?"

The silence following her question tormented her, reminding her of Lachlan. She strained to hear if he was still behind her, and heard nothing. Still, she wasn't alone.

She gestured around her. "I feel my parents in the warmth of the sun, hear them in the whisper of the wind, and see them in the silhouette of the tall pine. Unfortunately, I also sense them here"—she pointed down the throat of the cave—"where striving to reach them might lead to nothing but heartache."

"I reach only for Paris." Alexandre lifted his lantern high and peered once again into the darkness. "To secure my place there, I must achieve a triumph here. With my grand discovery and your honest beauty, no one will deny my rise to greatness. Together we shall take Paris by storm. Stay with me and you will learn how true success is achieved."

She might not find a life partner in either man who'd followed her from Fort Shelton, but she could gain insight from whatever came next. "I hope to learn many truths today."

"Be careful what you wish for." Lachlan's warning rumbled behind her, deep and earnest.

He'd stayed. Her blood raced, flooding her with the futile hope he'd stand by her forever.

"Why are you still here, Tracker? Mademoiselle Rousseau said she wanted to be far away from you. I am of the same mind."

Lachlan's tall, broad frame filled her view. Shoulders squared and feet planted wide, he stood in front of her with his back to the cave. "Before you continue, you must learn what attacked me."

"A bear. Nothing more. End of story." Alexandre's lantern creaked as his arm swung in an irate arc, sending light everywhere but illuminating nothing.

Lachlan stood stone-still. "A beast lumbered toward me on all fours, then rose on its hind legs."

"As a bear does," Alexandre hissed.

"It spoke in a familiar voice. Recalled my past. Recited my failures."

A wintry memory raised gooseflesh on Élodie's skin. "A spirit walker."

Alexandre's voice rose with incredulity. "A fairy tale that only frightens children."

"It cursed me," Lachlan said.

"*It*," Alexandre shot back, "has nothing to do with my cave."

"It's lodged in this rock and inside my head. I've carried it with me for the last four months. It calls me tr—"

"Tracker. *En quoi est-ce différent?* I call you Tracker. I imagine everyone does at some point."

What others said didn't matter. Not when Lachlan was finally opening up to her. "You speak of one voice?" she asked, wanting to encourage him to keep sharing.

Lachlan's lips flattened into an ominous line. "Always the same. The voice of my ghost."

"*C'est inventé de toute pièces,*" Alexandre muttered. "None of this is real."

An echo from the past rose in her mind. "I've heard it, too."

Alexandre gaped at her. "His madness has overtaken you. This conversation must end now. We continue. He goes away."

She leaned toward Lachlan. She couldn't let him leave. Not when a single word might make all the difference. "The day I found you, I heard a scream. I thought it cried the word *traitor,* but I couldn't be sure. I assumed it was you."

"Might've been. I can no longer tell what comes from inside or out."

The air from the cave smelled crisp with only a hint of damp. The putrid stench from before was gone, but that didn't mean the danger had gone with it. She shot a glance at a suddenly quiet Alexandre. "We require reinforcements. Gray Owl is familiar with the spirit world. I can find him and bring him back."

"*Non,*" Alexandre growled with a decisive shake of his head. "This is my discovery. More people will only dilute my success."

Lachlan surveyed the sky and the length of the shadows cast by the trees.

"What are you staring at?" Alexandre demanded.

"It's getting late in the day. We should wait till tomorrow."

"Tomorrow my team will arrive." Alexandre's gaze skewered Lachlan. "Is that why you followed me?"

Lachlan gave an exasperated snort. "I followed her, not you."

"And sly as a fox, you waited. When the cave consumed my attention, you engaged her in whispers to hide your plans for me."

"Lachlan did not start that conversation. I did."

Alexandre's glare cut to her. "Did he tell you my team was already at the fort?"

"He did not."

"Did he say that they paid him to delay my progress until they could catch up? He hopes they already have. This is why he looks downhill." Alexandre scanned the mountain below. *"Je vois quelque chose dans les arbres!"*

She wished she saw someone in the trees as well. That Gray Owl had returned. That any one of the strong men and women who'd rallied around her to form a family stood nearby. "You see only the wind rippling the leaves and shifting the shadows. The one thing out of the ordinary sits above us."

"Encore un ramassis d'absurdités. More manipulations and lies!" Alexandre spun around and dove into the black rift.

"Wait!" Élodie leapt after him.

Lachlan latched on to her arm and held her fast. "You cannot stop him, but you can help him. What did you see?"

"Something that wasn't here four months ago." She grasped his arm as well and drew him away from the cave. Standing on the edge of the outcrop, she pointed upward. "There. Halfway between us and the peak. A gap in the previously smooth wall of firs."

"A small break. Only a few trees have fallen."

"Or the earth beneath collapsed."

Lachlan stiffened, but his hold on her remained gentle. "An entrance to another cave?"

"The spirit walker could've moved there. Before I found you, it acknowledged my presence with an irritable snort. It also chose to go to ground and leave me unharmed."

"You're hoping it might behave similarly with Duval." His tone carried no conviction.

"Or that it's burrowed deep enough in this mountain I won't even meet it this time."

"You mean *we* won't. I'm staying by your side, remember?"

A wave of pure joy propelled her toward him. She wrapped her arms around his waist and laid her head against the sturdy wall of his chest. "We're stronger together."

Beneath her touch, his muscles tensed, hard-

ening to iron. She steeled herself for the disappoint-
ment of him pushing her away.

His breath brushed the top of her hair. "You're
strong. I'm not." His heart thudded hard and fast
against her ear. "The voice has wormed deep into my
soul, leaching my sanity and strength. Duval is right.
I'm a walking corpse."

"No, you are alive. You've battled your voice on
your own for months and survived." She tightened
her grip on him. She wasn't letting him go. "Today
you will not fight alone. Tell me when it speaks to
you, and I will share your burden."

Lachlan's arms enveloped her and removed the
distance separating them. "There is more to share
than what it says."

A yelp echoed inside the cave.

She raised her head and her lantern toward the
blackness. She didn't want to set one foot outside of
Lachlan's embrace, but she must. "Tell me inside."

CHAPTER 4

Lachlan cursed his lack of foresight. If he'd taken the time to replace the rifle strap that his attacker had shredded four months ago, he could've slung his Winchester over his arm and pulled Élodie even closer.

His arms refused to function. He couldn't let go. Not when holding Élodie made him feel both alive and safe. One clear choice remained for bettering her safety. Move before she did. Transferring his hold from woman and weapon to only the latter, he leapt into the abyss.

The cold dark swallowed him. Not even the tip of his Winchester was visible as he sighted along the barrel.

A heartbeat later, Élodie's lantern cast a circle of light around him. The warmth of her body stayed close as they crept forward in absolute silence. She'd make a first-rate fugitive tracker if she decided to stop guiding and start hunting.

Today she did both. She'd crossed into his nightmare.

Whatever monstrous shape it took—bear, man, or spirit walker—it wielded the power to spill her blood and snuff out her life. This time he could not hesitate. He must pull the trigger. And if bullets failed, he must use his body. Whatever lay ahead would have to shred him to pulp before it laid a claw on Élodie.

He kept moving and staring dead ahead. He could no longer sidestep the second way to protect her. Tell her everything that lurked in his mind, no matter how mad. Give her the knowledge necessary to save herself. Accept damnation in the eyes of the woman he loved and who said she loved him. Once a horror surfaced, it could not be buried again.

That would come later. One did not talk while hunting, unless one wished to become the hunted.

A volley of familiar French curses punctured the silence. The words sounded a lot better when he'd heard them flowing from Élodie's lips.

Duval's impatience echoed in the dark, coming from everywhere. Lachlan swallowed his own frustration along with his warning for Duval to shut up or at least tell them something useful—like his location.

The Frenchman wouldn't listen. Golden Boy was too busy blustering and making himself a target Lachlan struggled to locate. He tightened his grip on his rifle and put one foot in front of the other.

Élodie's lantern revealed rough rock on either side. The cave had narrowed to a tunnel.

Her hand seized his elbow and tugged him to a halt. "You can lower your rifle. There's nothing ahead but Monsieur Duval."

"How can you be certain? I can't see a thing. Not even him."

"He's fallen." Her light swept downward, leading the way.

He dropped to one knee.

A rift stretched between the walls, angled to make it difficult to detect but still wide enough to prevent stepping or even jumping over. Duval stood at the bottom, adjusting his pack and brushing dirt from his clothing. His lantern lay at his feet. The light had died, but the metal and glass remained intact.

Duval was damned lucky he hadn't broken it or his neck.

Élodie's light moved again, scanning the sides.

The stone plummeted unnaturally straight like a pickaxe and chisel had been used to increase its height and reduce its roughness to the point where whoever fell in couldn't climb out. A considerable amount of work had been invested to block the path. The hand of man had left a heavy imprint here.

Élodie had told him she'd learned of the cave from a prospector. Had he or another made this excavation? Where were the bones the man had claimed to see? If one didn't count Duval, the cavity was devoid of both the dead and the waiting to die.

He stretched out on his stomach and extended his hand. "Toss up your lantern. You come next."

With a glare, Duval did as told. Lachlan caught the lantern, handed it to Élodie, and reached down again. Duval took a running leap and grabbed hold of him.

Golden Boy's weight yanked hard on his arm. His name took on a new meaning. A Federal Reserve vault might be lighter.

Lachlan gritted his teeth and heaved the man upward. Sweat broke out on his brow. Pain pricked, then flared in familiar points in his flesh. Élodie grasped Duval's coat collar and pulled with him.

Duval reached the top and flopped out, puffing and huffing like a trout on a riverbank.

Lachlan eased onto his side and lay still. His pain found a home in his ribs, stabbing deep and robbing him of breath. One minute of pulling had undone four months of healing. He'd torn an old wound.

A vision leaned over him. A woman enveloped in a halo highlighting the infinite shades of her dark blonde hair. Hair once so fair it led to her name

Yellow Feather. His heart lurched. The legend paled next to the woman.

Élodie used her lantern to inspect him. "Where did you get hurt?"

Her question ignited his pride and prodded him to his feet. The pain in his side flared before ebbing to a pulsing throb. "Shouldn't you be asking Duval?"

She arched one brow, challenging his evasiveness before she faced the Frenchman.

He stood as well and raked his fingers through his hair, combing it back into order. "I am perfectly fine."

With a nudge of his foot, Lachlan pushed Duval's lantern toward him. "You should light this. It'll do more good than reassembling your *perfect* appearance."

Duval's hands fell to his sides in fists. "At least I have one to reassemble."

Lachlan braced himself against throwing a punch or receiving one. "Whatever you *have*, I didn't see it getting you out of that pit. Nor will it take you across."

"I shall find a way before you do." Duval's dark eyes assessed him. "You teeter on the precipice of collapse."

"And yet I still stand while you fell."

"If you had not stolen my guide," Duval growled through gritted teeth, "I would not—"

"Gentlemen," Élodie interrupted in a winter-crisp voice. "I have made promises to help both of you. Today we proceed together, or not at all." She moved to stand on the boundary of the obstacle.

Lachlan went with her. Behind him, Duval's lantern scraped stone before its glow joined Élodie's. The narrowness of the corridor bunched them together, with her in the middle.

Duval's eyes flitted everywhere without pausing to take in a single thing—including the faint indents in the wall closest to him. "There must be a way across," he muttered.

"Let us know when you find it." Lachlan leaned against the opposite wall and prayed Duval wouldn't see anything, including his dwindling fortitude.

"The distance between us widens again." Élodie's hand clasped his. "Will you tell him, or is it up to me?"

The comfort of her touch made his answer leap from his lips. "Someone has carved hand and footholds into the rock to provide a crossing."

Duval's gaze moved incessantly. "Where?"

"On the wall nearest to you." He gestured with his chin.

"There's nothing there."

"You'd see more if you slowed down."

Duval's glower found him and didn't move. "Once again you *see* things that are not real. A man who believes in ghosts is not reliable."

"Anyone with a lick of sense would agree this hole is a warning to turn back."

"Did your imaginary voice tell you that?"

"Both of you would do better if you stopped dwelling in the past," Élodie scolded in a voice worthy of a schoolmarm.

Had she learned the tone from her adoptive mother, Faith Feather? He'd wondered before, but had hesitated to ask. Élodie was wrong. He hadn't learned everything about her. He hadn't made the most of their time together.

Her hand squeezed his gently. "Are you still with me?"

Although familiar, her patience still held the power to astound him. As did her impulsiveness. He'd bet his Winchester that Duval had yet to witness the latter trait in full force. His Élodie was as volatile as the volcanic rift that formed these mountains. She'd alternated between badgering and cajoling him. From the day she'd found him to every day afterward as she hauled him to Fort Shelton and then presided over his recovery.

Stay with me. Don't you dare die. I'm determined to teach you a new way to live.

He had one day left to show her she hadn't wasted her time. He pushed away from the wall. He clasped her hand tighter and extended his other arm to tap his Winchester's muzzle against each indent.

Duval was quick to use them, but on the other side he crept forward a lot more slowly. Maybe he'd heard Lachlan's warning to slow down. Whatever the case, Duval didn't pause to engage in further conversation or even glance back.

Élodie's hand slipped from his. With her carbine strap over her arm and her lantern tied to her rifle stock, she made her own crossing. His hands shot out, ready to catch her should she slip.

The moment her feet touched the other side, she untied her lantern and held its light his way. Her eyes widened when she saw him reaching out to her, then she smiled. Her happiness, combined with the fact that she had her back to the tunnel, made him scramble across faster than either her or Duval.

They crept forward as before, him with rifle raised, her close behind with her light. The only thing new was the pain biting his side as well as his leg.

"See?" she whispered. "The three of us can work well together."

His misgivings about Duval's solidarity died on his lips when Jellon's unflattering opinion of Lachlan's abilities hissed in his ear.

Unreliable wretch.

He'd promised to tell her when his voice returned. Before he could, a ghostly shroud covered the darkness, halting his words but not his steps.

With Duval somewhere ahead and Élodie close behind, there could be no going back.

The pale haze solidified into individual objects. Some round. Others cylindrical. All stacked to form tall piles covered in dust and cobwebs and a grim reality he couldn't shield Élodie from seeing.

He led her into a corridor lined with bones.

CHAPTER 5

É lodie's gaze darted left and right, up and down, never stopping, always hoping—and now also dreading. The prospector had described many bones, but not this never-ending sea. Poised like waves, the stacks reached Lachlan's shoulders and topped her head. Cobwebs torn by Alexandre's passage rained down. Dust motes disturbed by their feet rose up.

Her breath rasped loudly in the stifling hush. Not even pressing her palm over her mouth helped. She couldn't control her heart from racing in search of her parents.

Too many remains rested here. Too many to scour and find the ones she needed. Too many to come from whatever fell into the trap behind them. They'd walked into the lair of a hunter and a collector.

If they hadn't freed Alexandre, would his bones have joined these piles?

Her chest constricted. Her steps faltered. Lachlan moved a pace ahead, then another, leaving her in a rapidly narrowing tunnel of gray.

Her knees struck stone. The earth lurched up to meet her.

A hand grasped her arm and guided her down gently. She pressed her face to her knees. Her head found a home on the blessed firmness of her mountain. Even better, Lachlan's hand stayed on her arm.

"I'm here." His voice sounded muffled and faraway, but the warmth of his body came closer, shielding her. "You're not alone."

"I can't find them," she whispered back.

He released a resigned sigh. "And you may never."

"An intelligent person would give up."

"I'm glad you didn't. If you had, I'd never have met you."

His declaration eased the weight bearing down on her, but only for a moment. "We shouldn't be talking. The spirit walker will hear us."

"It will hear Duval first, and so will we." His hand rubbed her arm. "There's time for questions. And answers."

"Why did we meet? What brought you to my mountain?"

"Duty."

The word cast a gloomy chill over her and kept her huddled on the ground. "There must be more."

"Pride. Shame. Regret." His reply came in staccato bursts, then poured out fast like a floodgate had been opened. "I should've found Jellon. There was an opportunity, but it meant—" His breath hissed above her. "Shooting a young woman whose only crime was having brothers who became outlaws. The brothers captured Jellon. Their sister might've known his location, but she ran the second she saw me. A moving target is hard to stop."

She nodded with sudden understanding. "Fear often makes a runner dart unexpectedly. It can turn even a warning shot lethal. You were right to hesitate."

"But I was wrong to fail the man who taught me everything I once deemed gospel. In the end, I couldn't even find his body. Not even after six years."

"Like my parents, he's gone. But we can't stop searching. We need to understand how they died."

"What if we focused on how they lived?" He lifted her into a sitting position. He also kept her close. Her lantern lay somewhere nearby. Its hazy glare cast a hard light on Lachlan's scars and the clear blue of his eyes.

Tried and tested. Unwavering. He'd never walk away from her. Not inside this cavern or in any land beyond. That truth held her as securely as his gaze.

"I'm certain your parents lived well. They

taught you compassion and love. Jellon taught me to hunt, to never stop, to do whatever it took. His words tear me apart. Your parents' words raise you up."

A wry smile tugged her lips. "Hard to believe you didn't see me cowering on the ground a moment ago."

He blinked in surprise. Then a low chuckle escaped him. "I assumed you'd merely bent to retrieve something. Duval might've dropped that journal he's always scribbling in." His tone went from teasing to solemn. "Your parents' light will never leave you."

"But I left them." She closed her eyes tightly. The memory of Lachlan shutting his eyes against her assurances made her open hers fast. "I ventured into the woods for longer periods. I couldn't resist the lure of seeing new things."

"You were a fearless six-year-old."

"What if I hadn't left that day? Or come home sooner instead of staying out till all I saw was shadows?"

"You question whether you could've stopped whatever took them away." He paused as if weighing the probability before saying, "It's possible but not likely."

She scanned his face, wondering if all of her answers lay there.

"The odds were greater of you being hurt or

killed while your parents watched. If that had happened, their light might've clouded."

An icy chill crept up her spine. "More vengeful spirit walkers."

"I've spent my life hunting people who take lives as easily as property or money. They're hard to catch. Impossible to understand. I wish I'd invested more time searching for good people like you. I wish I could find your parents." He exhaled another long breath. "I can't. The only thing I can see in this corridor are animal bones."

The truth in his words made it easier to breathe. A human skull was too distinctive to be missed. "You'd tell me if you saw differently? You'll keep talking to me?"

He nodded. "I'll also remind you that a person was here. Only a human hand could assemble these piles."

"Same as the hole behind us." Her eyes raced left and right again. "Another trap. This one meant to distract or paralyze." She found her rifle and lantern and scooped them up.

Lachlan remained still, head cocked, listening. "We need to keep moving."

Her muscles clenched, ready to run.

"More than anything, we need to stay together." He pulled her to her feet. "Hold tight to my shirt. Let me be your eyes for these next steps."

With her fingers knotted in the back of his shirt,

her head found another home against his spine. She focused on timing her steps with his so they traveled swiftly. She'd counted fifty strides before he stopped.

"We're clear. We've also caught up with Duval."

She released her hold on Lachlan and claimed a spot beside him. The tunnel was now devoid of not only bones but the previously endless black ahead. They faced a wall of rocks stacked to obstruct their way. The air smelled stale and lay heavy on her skin. Like them, it had nowhere to go.

With his back to them, Alexandre knelt, staring not at the blockade but at a gap in the ground between him and the rock pile. A second steep-sided hole. Minus the carved indents necessary for crossing. No way forward. Nothing to want to reach on the other side.

Alexandre slumped against the nearest wall. With his chin on his chest, his groan rumbled deep with a familiar frustration, but also despair. "This is my grand discovery? My life is one colossal farce." He shook his fist in the air. "I am consigned to a world of futility crafted by lunatics wishing to render me equally insane. Why go to the effort of digging these pits when there is nothing ahead to guard?"

A half-smile curved Lachlan's lips as he watched her. "A good question. What's our answer?"

Her heart leapt under his warm regard and also his desire to continue speaking with her. "There must be something still ahead."

He nodded, but frowned at the hole. "And only one way to reach it."

She stretched out on her stomach—the same way Lachlan had when he'd pulled Alexandre from the first obstacle. Lachlan joined her. They lay side by side, peering down while she used her lantern to reveal stone as uniform and steep as the first excavation, but also twice as deep. The light barely touched the bottom and left the corners in shadows.

One opportunity had been hammered into the rock. An iron spike with a ring on the end lay within arm's reach. Her gaze shot to Lachlan.

He stared at the ring like it was the devil. "I'm hearing my voice again."

His bleak tone made her heart ache. "What does it say?"

"Nothing good. I'm an idiot for even considering climbing in, but also a coward for hesitating." He extended his hand to Alexandre. "We need your rope."

Alexandre shot forward, pushing Lachlan's hand aside so he could sprawl on the ground beside them. This time he required no prompting or pointing. "A climber's pin," he whispered like a gleeful child.

"Or a miner's," Lachlan added. "It probably hauled up rock to block the tunnel."

It probably also lifted bones from a hidden dining chamber. She kept the comment to herself. Lachlan had his own voice pestering him. And more than anyone, he knew how depraved a soul they might find when they passed the last of its traps and tests of fortitude.

Without doffing his pack, Alexandre freed his rope. Using an economy of movement, he tied it to the pin, swung over the side, and started lowering himself.

Lachlan grabbed his arm.

Alexandre's glare shot upward. "What is the delay now?"

"Thought you might want this." Lachlan held down Alexandre's lantern.

"When I reach the bottom, tie it to the line and winch it down." Alexandre flashed an unexpected grin. "Don't want it to break."

"Sounds wise."

"Try not to sound so surprised." As Alexandre moved downward, his voice bubbled upward, buoyant with excitement and a returning confidence. "We have mountains in France. And I have scaled more of them than all of the academics on my team combined."

As soon as Alexandre's boots touched the bottom, he dropped into a crouch and pivoted in a circle. He stopped suddenly to study the ground again. This time on their far left.

Well," Lachlan drawled, "he hasn't reached for his revolver yet. That's a good sign."

"Are you ready for your lantern now?" Élodie called softly.

"Or do you prefer the rope left down in case you need a swift exit?"

"*Allez, envoyez-la maintenant!*" Without looking up, Alexandre waved his hand above his head. "Hurry. Send down the lantern."

When they did, the light revealed a low crevice. Impossible to see inside from their vantage point. Alexandre had the perfect view, but he'd once again gone as silent and still as the stone around them.

"I'm beginning to appreciate how vexing you found my silences," Lachlan muttered before calling down to Alexandre, "Any chance of sharing what you see?"

"A crawl space." Alexandre doffed his pack and yanked out his canvas wrapped bundle. With his lantern in one hand and the bundle in the other, he crawled on his belly into the crack and disappeared.

"How unlike him not to wait for us," Lachlan quipped as he slid over the edge and began his descent. "Don't bother to winch down my rifle."

He'd left his Winchester beside her. Unlike her carbine, it didn't have a carry strap, and he needed both hands on the rope.

"Toss it down. I'll catch it."

After she did, his smile of thanks fell into a frown as he stared up at her.

"Tell your voice," she said as she looped her

carbine over her arm in preparation for her climb, "to go straight back to hell if it's suggesting either of us is safer on our own. We know better." She tied her lantern to the end of her rifle so the flat stock lay between her clothing and the flame's heat. No one was left to relay the light down to her.

But someone stood below to catch her. She didn't have to look to know Lachlan's hands would be raised and ready.

When she reached his side, they dropped as one to their knees to peer into the crevice. Lachlan had both hands firmly on his Winchester again. She thrust her lantern as far as she could into the fissure while he crawled in and scrambled up to stand in a space beyond.

He took several seconds to adjust his stance, which told her his leg was still bothering him. And his side as well. He uttered not s single complaint. Not even a grunt. She sealed her lips against inquiring how poorly he felt. Even injured, he was stronger than most of Fort Shelton's residents. And those folks were darned tough.

Only Lachlan's feet remained visible, and just barely in the gloom.

Before she could ask what he saw, he spoke. "Too dark to see, but I can feel more grooves for climbing."

"Do you hear anything?"

"Like Duval? No, he's scampered off like the

expert climber he claimed to be. I'm not moving till you're beside me. Be prepared to get cozy."

When she crawled through and stood up, the cramped space brought her chest flat against his. His heart beat fast against her, but his gaze remained frozen, sighting up the barrel of his Winchester into the blackness above. He reached for a handhold, preparing to pull himself up and away from her.

She reached up as well. She clasped his face between her palms and drew him down to face her. "You're a good person. If *any* voice says otherwise, they're wrong."

His eyes narrowed dubiously but didn't close.

She pulled him closer until their noses nearly touched. "Your friend Jellon didn't understand you like I do."

"He was my mentor. He knew me longest."

"That doesn't mean he knew you well. *Zut, alors!* He's the one who told you to kill or be killed, isn't he? *Quel tyran.* I'm glad you chose your own path."

"I had no path till I met Jellon. I have no memories of my mother, but I'll never forget the bite of hunger under my father's rule as overseer of a trading post in the far north. He drank. I stole food. I spent more time in the company hoosegow than out. A mountain of a man arrived. Dragged in one thief and hauled another out. Did it on a dare that he couldn't turn a runt like me into a man. Jellon Jerome always was a legend."

Now that she wasn't distracted by fear, a memory sprang to mind. Jellon Jerome's name had come with the gossip that followed Lachlan. "Did he miss his glory days as the only legend?"

A frown pinched his brow. "He never missed a thing."

"Some say you eventually arrested more criminals than him. You outshone him."

He tried to pull away, but there was nowhere to go. "No. Maybe. Only after he was gone."

"Like Alexandre he craved a grand achievement. A lone conquest." Her attention darted upward, but only briefly. The most important person stood in her grasp. "That's why the man you call mentor didn't wait for your help. He decided he had to catch those outlaws on his own."

"They cut off his hand. I found it in a mining shaft similar to this. Six years later, I came to your mountain, stood below this hellhole, and listened to his voice bellowing from a beast covered in fur and claws. He's the spirit walker."

"Whatever he is, you're stronger than him."

He bowed his head. His forehead touched hers, but he didn't close his eyes. "You forget how you found me. My defeat was complete that day."

She slid her fingers into his hair, searching for the scars she knew lay hidden there. "Do you remember me telling you why I'm drawn to scars?"

He nodded. "Your parents were doctors. They

transformed wounds into scars and, in doing so, saved lives."

"To me, scars are a badge of victory. They mean both doctor and patient won the battle to heal." With great reverence, she pressed a kiss to each of his cheeks and his scars. "But what of the battle that led to the wounds?"

He stiffened as if that fight were upon him. "I can never recall it clearly."

"Tell me what you remember."

"A humped blur of fur surged out of the blackness. With a roar, it lurched upright. Claws swung from its chest and flashed in rows on its limbs. It struck my face. Blinded me with my own blood. Loomed over me in an endless rage. Slashing and snarling. Its voice broke into my head and never left."

"But you survived."

"The ground beneath me crumbled, and I fell into a silent, snowy white. Then I heard your voice speaking of bravery and awoke to an even greater nightmare." A condemned look clouded his eyes. "I became the beast."

"No." She shook him hard enough to bring his focus back to her. "You stayed true to yourself."

"Truth is, I don't know who I am."

"I do. I felt your Winchester against my heart and watched you struggle to do what you'd been taught. You hesitated. You lowered your weapon. You did the same with that innocent woman you said might've helped you find Jellon. Tell me, did you hesitate to use your rifle against the spirit walker as well?"

He went stiff as a board in her grasp. "That was inexcusable weakness."

"Isn't there strength in doing what we suspect will cause us pain? I chose to hesitate as well."

His eyebrows shot up. "You could've shot it?"

"More importantly, I could've shot you. If hesitating makes you weak, then I'm weak as well. But can it be that simple when life is infinitely complicated? I don't believe so. I've been taught differently."

His voice deepened as if reciting a solemn prayer. "Never shoot until you see, with clear eyes, what you might kill. I choose bravery."

It was her turn to be surprised. "You said you couldn't recall that day clearly. How can you remember what I said word for word?"

"Your words gave me hope. I dreamed of a day when I might be one of your choices. It's been my greatest wish for the last four months."

And hers as well. Soft laughter echoed around her, rising and falling, bubbling with joy. It came from deep within her and from high above—in the dark shaft and whatever lay beyond.

Alexandre's laughter mingled with hers, sounding like he'd also received his heart's desire. He'd found his grand discovery that would allow him to reach Paris. He'd be ready to leave this cave now. And so could she and Lachlan. A clear path shone in her mind for the three of them having their hopes fulfilled.

But first, there was time for words.

She stared into a pair of pale blue eyes that held the only light she needed. "Hesitation, patience, bravery. I choose them all. And I see them all in you. So, yes, I choose you, Lachlan Bravery."

CHAPTER 6

"I doubt you'll find a drop of patience in me right now." Lachlan fought the urge to kiss Élodie and never stop. "All I can think about is getting you out of this cave so I can show you exactly how much I adore you."

Élodie's grin grew, making the darkness inside him retreat even further. "Do your plans include kissing me?"

"Definitely."

"Well, let's get moving. The sooner we do, the sooner we can have our kiss." Her fingers slid through his hair and down his face as if unable to stop touching him. At the last possible second, she let go.

As soon as she did, he pulled himself up and away. The only way he could was the certainty she'd be close behind him, or rather below. Her lantern glowed near his feet, barely making a dent in the dark.

Suddenly he wasn't worried if everything went pitch black. He had new words filling his head and lighting his way. *I choose you, Lachlan Bravery.*

Élodie made him see a glimmer of good inside him. She made not only his scars but his future seem beautiful.

Above him, another light appeared. A second glow made by a flickering lantern flame. If it belonged to Duval, why didn't the man call down the shaft and advise them what lay ahead? Was he being self-absorbed again? Or was he lying beside his lantern, unable to move or even speak?

He reached the top and didn't stop. He leapt out to stand, legs braced, Winchester raised, ready for combat. When his injuries protested his heroics, he struggled not to stagger.

He needn't have bothered. Nothing pounced on him. No one required assistance or even acknowledged his arrival.

Two strides to his right, Duval sat scribbling in his journal. His lantern rested above his head on a rock pile that fell in a jumble to form a throne of stone. They'd reached the other side of the blockade.

Duval's canvas wrapped bundle was now stuffed in the coat pocket that previously held his journal. Why had he chosen to bring the package with him instead of leaving it in his discarded pack?

"What is it?" Standing close beside him, Élodie's voice was hushed with awe.

He wondered the same. Her gaze was not on Duval, however, but the new tunnel arcing around them.

He would've had to multiply his height by three to touch the top. The width sprawled twice that. Nothing measured up to the stone's undulating, ropy surface. On a gradual incline, the ripples flowed as far as he could see with hardly a break in their amazingly unvarying geography.

The hands of a giant—or the body of a behemoth worm—would've been necessary to form a channel this large and uniform.

Duval's eyes shifted from his journal to his subject, then back again. Always moving. Along with his pencil. "This is a lava tube formed by a long ago eruption."

Élodie laid her palm reverently on the nearest wall. "It's magical."

"Caves such as this have definitely cast a spell over my society. The rewards bestowed for their discovery have been *phénoménales*. Beyond that, there is no magic. Only science. When magma from the Earth's core surfaces through a vent, it streams downhill. The outside cools and hardens while the hotter interior continues to flow. Eventually, everything ends. This hollow is left in its wake."

"Your find is indeed a grand one." Élodie's gaze left

the stone and found Lachlan. Her smile grew and lit up her whole face. "We've all been well-rewarded today."

His heart leapt and his smile joined hers.

"I had hoped this cave would be larger. God willing, it shall be sufficient to satisfy my benefactors." Although Duval's words were swift, they weren't rushed. Neither was his focus on his sketching. The man appeared to have at least one thing that settled his impatience.

Being this close to Élodie while she beamed at him gave him a glimpse of his own serenity. It also doubled his impatience. He yearned to swap one secluded place for another so he could begin exploring every facet of Élodie's love.

"Mademoiselle Rousseau, I need you to proceed to either end of the tube. I must insert your height into my drawing for scale."

Lachlan fell into step beside her. He stole a glance at Duval's creation as they walked by. In only a few minutes, he'd fashioned a masterpiece full of texture and nuance.

"Stay out of the picture." Duval's arm shot out like a gate to halt Lachlan's progress with Élodie. His other hand hovered over his journal, pencil raised and unmoving.

Its scribbling still disturbed the air. Rasping and scraping. Eerily echoing from every direction, but also concentrated in the downward slope's deep blackness.

"Only the mademoiselle is needed." Duval's grating tone drowned out everything else and yanked Lachlan's attention back to him.

He shoved Duval's arm aside. "You're crazier than me if you think I'll let her face this cavern's shadows alone."

Duval raised a condescending eyebrow. "Still frightened of your *croque-mitaine?*"

"My what?"

"Your mitten-biter. Although I suppose some might say hand-cruncher." With a shrug, he resumed his drawing.

The pairing of his pencil with the rustling in the shadows grated like fingernails on slate and raised Lachlan's hackles.

"What the blazes are you talking about?" he demanded.

"He speaks of a bugbear." Élodie's voice had gone chill as a northern gale. "A goblin that eats naughty children. Once again, he belittles our concerns about a spirit walker."

"*C'était une blague,* Mademoiselle."

"Your joke was unnecessary, Monsieur. And more importantly, unkind."

"*Mon Dieu!* You are easily offended. And riled. I had not noticed this trait before."

That's because you were a fool who didn't bother to

look. Even now the Frenchman didn't, but Lachlan did and was rewarded with a magical sight.

Élodie in a high rage. Eyes blazing in his defense.

"You should speak more kindly to people who go out of their way to help you. Lachlan deserves your respect."

"I would respect him immensely if he kept his size out of my picture." Without raising his eyes from his drawing, Duval swept his hand over Lachlan, from heel to head and back again. "He will make my lava tube appear smaller than it already is."

With an irate growl, Élodie spun away from Duval to face him. "He's intolerably self-centered. He —" Her jaw dropped and her shoulders relaxed. Her fury departed as quickly as it came. "Why are you looking at me like that?"

"Because you are my shining light, while Duval isn't a very bright one." Such clarity in the midst of many shadows had him smiling and frowning at the same time. "Whatever his brilliance, we are stronger together."

"I'm finding him increasingly difficult to assist." Her teeth tugged her lower lip. "Or even understand."

His gaze locked on her mouth, eager to kiss her until neither one of them could think straight, let alone worry.

"However..." A slow smile bowed her mouth.

"My belief in you and me sharing a lovely harmony grows stronger."

"I believe we need to hurry up and get out of here." He tore his focus away from her and kicked the toe of Duval's boot.

The action had the desired effect.

Duval's eyes rose from his journal to challenge him. "What do you want now?"

"To learn how many drawings you require before we can leave."

"At least one with Mademoiselle Rousseau added for perspective."

"You can forget about me leaving her side." He raised his palm when Duval opened his mouth to argue. "You're good at ignoring what you don't wish to see. Disregard my presence. Draw only her."

"*Quelle merveilleuse suggestion.*" Duval flicked his fingers dismissively. "Proceed."

Lachlan ignored the aching throb in his leg as he limped beside Élodie up the lava tube. He concentrated on placing his feet carefully so that he made no sound. He couldn't stop his eyes from darting forward and back, scanning the blackness looming at either end.

"*Arrêtez.* Halt there," Duval called in a raised voice.

Lachlan's gut protested the noise, but his legs followed the order. Answering Élodie's questions in the corridor of bones had been a necessary risk.

Continuing to speak, especially as loudly as Duval's just had, went against everything he knew to be wise. Yet he'd talked more here while facing his demons than he had in all the months hiding from them in Fort Shelton.

Unfortunately, if anything lurked in the shadows, it would acknowledge their intrusion sooner or later, and not in a friendly way.

A high but small circle of light disturbed the darkness ahead. Unlike the harsh yellow flames Élodie and Duval carried in their lanterns, this light didn't flicker. It glowed steady as a distant moon tinged with a pink that reminded him of Élodie's jacket.

The warmth of her arm brushed his and stayed. She would've had to release her rifle or lantern to clasp his hand. Instead, she kept a firm grip on both and, with her gaze pinned on the tunnel ahead, kept track of Lachlan by touch.

The wisdom and trust in the gesture humbled him. But the worry furrowing her brow had him speaking before thinking.

"What's wrong?" The number of answers to such a question made him grimace. The only thing right about their situation was being with her.

"There are no human bones here either. No bones of any sort."

He resumed his search for anything beyond the uniform stone broken only by the shadows at its ends, the faint light and the rock pile marking their entry point. Any number of nooks and crannies—and passageways like the one they'd used—might be hidden in the gloom. Or there might be nothing more.

"Could your prospector have got confused with another cave?"

"Doubtful. Old-timers like him possess the directional abilities of a bat. Like the ones down there." She used her chin to gesture behind her. "The bats, I mean."

He nodded. They were, of course, the most logical source of the rustling. He needed to focus. Bats meant something else: another way in and out of here.

Any number of paths could lead a person to where they needed to go.

A sudden urge to learn more about Élodie's needs had him asking, "What did Duval say to encourage you to go with him to France?"

"It wasn't one thing. He spoke of forming a team of two with a future that never stayed still. We'd travel to St. Louis, Chicago, and Boston." Her words tumbled out fast and breathless with excitement. "We'd board a ship. Sail across an ocean. Tour Paris. Present his grand discovery together." She paused to draw in air before finishing in a hushed tone, "Continue east to Lyon."

She'd told him that her parents had left Lyon

after they'd been disowned for marrying against their families' wishes.

"You want to learn more about your ancestors."

"I have a craving to walk in their footsteps across the Volcanic Velay. Or the mountain of hell, as Monsieur Duval more often calls them. But like here, they are dormant."

The rustling at the opposite end of the lava tube grew louder. The bats were awakening with a hunger to fly and feed.

"Nothing sleeps forever. Did he suggest that your grandparents would welcome you?"

"If he had, I wouldn't have believed him. That outcome is unlikely. Still, I yearn to make the journey. Monsieur Duval only said we'd be good partners. We share certain similarities."

Lachlan scanned her instead of the lava tube. "But you are nothing alike."

One of her eyebrows shot up in challenge. "We are both driven to move forward. Impatiently so."

"He is nothing but impatient. And you must know..." He tucked a wayward strand of her hair behind her ear. It provided an excuse to touch her. "I have a desire to go with you." His hand hovered over her cheek, unwilling to return to his Winchester.

She nestled her face in the curve of his palm and finally met his gaze. "You're thinking about our kiss."

"Is it that obvious?"

"It's in your eyes. The way you watch me." She

pivoted to face him fully. "Like you want to devour me."

"That doesn't alarm you? In any way?"

"My only concern is that you keep a final barrier between us. You continue to hide your pain."

"Right now my pain is manageable. And with any luck, Duval won't fall into another hole and change that."

The scuff of footsteps—where Duval had previously sat silent—yanked his gaze from her while at the same time his hand pulled her closer. "He's on the move again."

"A bother and a blessing," Élodie replied with a sigh. "Besides you, there is only one thing I wish to get closer to right now."

"The sphere of light?"

"We remain in harmony."

"While Duval heads in the opposite direction."

With his lantern lifted toward the dark, Duval stopped abruptly and cocked his head as if straining to hear.

Lachlan concentrated on listening as well. Nothing rose above the rustling.

Duval set his lantern on the ground and opened the door to the flame. Then he pulled the bundle from his pocket.

"Damn him to hell and back." Lachlan pushed Élodie behind him. "Why would he want to blow up his discovery?"

"He doesn't. That's not dynamite. It only shares a similar size and shape. When I first noticed him adding it to his pack, I questioned him right away."

The perks of conversing became another shade clearer. "What is it then?"

Her arm settled against his again as she moved to his side. "It's an illumination flare specially designed by his society for searching below ground. I refused to go anywhere with him without a demonstration. The light blazed brighter than any I've seen. All without exploding."

Duval extracted a single stick and returned the others to his pocket.

"I hope you stood a safe distance away during such an exhibition."

Her snort of laughter eased his worries as much as her reply. "I most certainly did. I'm keeping the same distance here."

Duval touched his flare to his lantern's flame and raised the stick high above his head. The spark at its end burst into a blinding white that covered everything with its brightness.

A bellowing roar echoed off the walls. A torrent of high-pierced shrieks followed.

Fragments of black tore through the white light like buckshot from a gun. Hundreds of slender winged bodies screeched and darted. They obliterated Duval and his light from view as they swooped up the tunnel toward them.

Élodie stepped into his arms the instant he reached for her. He spun his back to the wave as they pulled each other to the ground. Lying face-to-face on their sides, he tucked her head under his chin and sheltered her with his body.

Gusts of air driven by many flapping wings swept him from head to heel. Nothing solid hit him. Even startled bats were swift enough to avoid anything that stood between them and wherever they wanted to go, which he imagined was their limitless freedom above ground.

"The light we observed must be a vent to the sky." Élodie's words warmed his chest where her lips hovered.

He pulled her closer.

The shrieking wave of wings ended abruptly. In its wake, the stench of old blood and bat excrement hit him. He released Élodie and jumped up to face the darkness that had swallowed not only Duval and his lantern but his flare.

The only illumination came from beside him. Élodie thrust her lantern toward the shadows, revealing a giant mass of fur racing toward them.

He jumped in front of her. With no time or space to fire a shot, he swung his Winchester like a club. His blow struck hard and jarred him as well as his target.

A howl of outrage battered his ears as the beast stumbled sideways. It lurched up to tower over him, huffing and snorting and tossing its head from side to side. The tips of its grizzled fur cut wild silver arcs in the narrow space separating them. So did a row of razor-sharp teeth below a bear's snout and a pair of unblinking eyes.

"Finally," the monstrosity rasped in a guttural growl. "I've caught you. Tell me where he went and where the other one hides. Speak or die."

CHAPTER 7

Lachlan kept his body between Élodie and the demon from his nightmares. "Don't come any closer. I won't let you lay a finger on her."

"How about a claw?" A handless arm punched a hole in the fur. With a mighty shove, it flipped its pelt over its hunched spine, revealing hundreds of claws sewn haphazardly into a long buckskin shirt stained with old rust-colored blood. The longest claws flared from stiff leather arm braces. One arm ended in a stump, the other in a man's hand.

Élodie's voice swept over him like a calming breeze. "Tell us who you seek, spirit walker."

"Give me the Bellamy Brothers!"

Lachlan wished he could, but the outlaws in question had swung long ago on the gallows. "Go back to the land of the dead. You'll find them there."

"I'll find them here and make you regret your lies."

"I speak the truth."

"You're still a traitor. One of those French bastards was just here."

Lachlan scanned his foe, searching for a way to defeat him.

His opponent lifted his head high and glared down at him as if seeking the same. Wearing a bear's head for a crown, Jellon Jerome's face loomed larger than Lachlan had ever recalled.

"How do you intend to stop me, boy? By waving your Winchester at me like a magician's wand? I'm not going to disappear this time." He circled left, strides swift and precise, the pace of a predator well versed in the hunt.

Lachlan moved with him. Falling into old sparring routines eased some of the fear gripping him. Not much, but maybe enough to mean the difference between a speedy death and lasting long enough to save Élodie.

The glow of her lantern's light followed him, assuring him she was still behind him.

"François and Tomas Bellamy told me you'd died."

"Another lie." Jellon kept circling. "I'm damned hard to kill. You know that. You also know your Winchester won't stop me."

Lachlan ignored Jellon's attempt to goad him on

a tender subject. The instant his attention wavered would be the moment Jellon attacked.

"You won't pull the trigger. You never do."

"Today I will."

A pitying look twisted Jellon's face. "Today is no different from any other."

"Today I'm not alone."

Jellon inhaled sharply. Hurt and fury flashed in his eyes. He had his own sensitive spot—the belief that Lachlan had abandoned him. With his next breath, Jellon feinted one way and leapt the other. He surged forward with his fingers and claws reaching for Élodie.

Lachlan's hand shot out as well. He punched Jellon in the jaw and sent him reeling. Jellon came up snarling and spitting blood. Lachlan kept his gaze on him but couldn't stop his impulse to reach back for solid proof that Élodie was still behind him.

Her hand grabbed his arm and held on tight.

Jellon's jaw dropped in disbelief. "This is why you let the Bellamy bitch go?" He stood frozen, staring wide-eyed at Élodie's hand on Lachlan's arm. "You besotted fool. You're in love with her."

"Who are the Bellamys?" Élodie asked in an undaunted voice. "I've never met anyone by that name."

"You're one and the same." Jellon resumed his circling, this time with a hunched spine and bared teeth.

Lachlan countered his movements. Élodie did the same. Her hand stayed on his arm, and her lantern light moved with them, which meant she'd transferred her rifle to her shoulder. She wasn't prepared to shoot Jellon, and despite Lachlan's words, he wasn't either.

"You're part of their despicable band of outlaws. And liars. And thieves!" Jellon shook the stump of his arm at her. "You're as responsible as your brothers for the loss of my hand."

A flinch of surprise shook Élodie's hold on him, but her voice remained steady. "Why does he think I'm the woman you wouldn't shoot six years ago?"

"Because he's no different from me. He's—" Lachlan stopped short of saying insane. He couldn't stop the accusation from roaring inside his head.

Her hand squeezed his arm. "He's letting his past cloud his decisions."

He drew in a deep breath as he reassessed his battle plan. Could he fight his mentor with the man's own words?

"*A skilled tracker shuns sentiment. He trusts his eyes.* If anyone looked closely, they'd see you cannot be Bernadette Bellamy. You look nothing alike."

"The Bellamys are all the same," Jellon hissed. "French devils with hair and eyes black as night."

"You're describing her opposite. *Look* at her."

"I am! She's different, yes, but so are you and I. Years have passed, but her face is still familiar."

"That's because you saw me only a few months ago," Élodie was quick to reply, "not many years ago."

"The last person who invaded my solitude was a man stooped with age and rattling with pickaxes and pans. He would've made a nice addition to my bone collection, but he fled so fast he didn't even see me chasing him. You're not him."

"I came the day after. We met outside this cavern, not inside."

Recognition widened Jellon's eyes. "You're the other hunter who couldn't pull a trigger."

"And you're the man who chose to walk away rather than continue to attack."

"Had I known you were a Bellamy, I'd have destroyed everything in my path to reach you." Jellon launched his entire body at Lachlan.

He scrambled back. Élodie's hand pulling his arm aided his retreat. She helped him avoid every claw but one. The tip tore a gash in his shirt. The skin beneath burned like wildfire as Jellon drew his arm back for another blow.

Without speaking to each other, he and Élodie moved as one, dodging his strikes. They saved their words for Jellon.

"She isn't Bernadette."

"My name is Élodie Rousseau."

"You're a Bellamy. Your accent keeps changing, hoping to hide your identity. But I still hear your

French." Jellon sped up his assault. The claws on his arms whistled through the air like hawks diving at mice.

"You hear her parents. They came from France, not Montreal."

"I don't care about her parents. I'm after her brothers."

"I have none. I have Eagle Feather and Faith, and all who call them friend. They gave me my voice."

"You're a woman used to lying her way out of anything, including a mining camp full of outlaws."

"She's never been beyond these mountains."

Jellon's next swipe grazed him from shoulder to elbow. He avoided worse by spinning hard to this right. The pain in his side—where Jellon had cut him months ago—stabbed deep and made his breath hiss between his teeth.

Jellon's laughter echoed off the walls. "What ails you, boy? Has your lack of courage and brains finally corrupted your body? You always were a spineless halfwit who never understood my wisdom."

"I understood. I just chose a different path."

"You chose wrong!" Jellon's rebuttal exploded like gunfire. "You're doing it again. A Bellamy has you hoodwinked. I can still hear them bragging about that feat." He halted with his arm lifted for another blow. He stared at a point above their heads, eyes glassy and unfocused. "On and on they went about how they'd not only outwitted me, but how their tiny sister had bested my famous protégé."

"I never stopped searching for you."

Jellon's eyes bulged like a toad's as he sank deeper into his memories. "When it mattered most, you were too slow. Even the reporter arrived faster. The story of my downfall would've raised their standing. Insignificant men made glorious. My name reduced to a laughingstock not only in the Colony of British Columbia but all the way north to the ice fields and south to the Rio Grande."

"Bernadette Bellamy was innocent of any wrongdoing, and her brothers paid dearly for the gold they stole and the lives they ruined. As did the members of their gang. They've hung for their crimes."

"One lives!" Jellon's gaze swooped down to pin him. "You followed him into my sanctuary."

"No, I captured every one of them and transported them to jail."

"You can't find anyone." Jellon raised the stump of his arm even higher. "Only I had the strength to do what needed to be done."

Like a slap to his head, a chilling realization hit Lachlan. "You cut off your own hand."

"Of course I did! They had me chained to a wall, and the axe was too dull to split iron. It was sharp enough for the reporter's neck. I picked up his pistol and downed every man who didn't run. The Bellamys ran the fastest."

"You ran as well," Élodie shot back in a scolding tone. "How could you let Lachlan live with the belief that you died?"

"When I came out of the mine, I met a blizzard. I staggered downhill only to fall into a cavern. Unlike my unreliable apprentice, I dispatched the bear inside with only one shot. She formed my table and bed as I waited for the storm to clear and my body to strengthen to the point where I'd never be taken prisoner again. I donned her fur and the first of my collection." He ran his hand reverently down his breastplate of claws.

"Why not search for me then?" Lachlan demanded.

"People are fickle. Their appreciation fleeting. I hunt only for monuments that stand the test of time."

"The stacks of bones." Élodie's voice was as hushed as it had been when surrounded by them. "Where are the others?"

A cunning look narrowed Jellon's eyes as he studied her. "Your interest in the macabre is strong. Tell me where your brothers are, and I'll show you the treasures I've buried."

Élodie snorted in disbelief. "Now you're lying. You don't hide bones. You put them on display."

"Not the human ones."

Lachlan's skepticism left him huffing as well.

"You always said men were no different from animals in life and in death."

"Didn't I also say a single man could create a world of chaos? If a prospector starts gossiping about a noteworthy find, the hordes will follow. You both arrived the day after my visitor."

Lachlan swallowed his retort. Élodie's arrival had been prompted by that visit, but arguing that the timing of his was a coincidence would be considered another lie.

"Too late," Jellon continued, "I discovered death, same as gold or silver, carries its own allure. After your arrival, I spent endless days rearranging bones and stones. Did it all with one hand." His voice grew gruffer and more guttural with each word. "I won. My solitude was restored. Then you chose to return." He raised his other arm as well and resumed stalking them. "Now I get to choose. No one leaves. Your bones will stay forever with mine."

Lachlan couldn't let that happen. He raised his Winchester.

Élodie's future shone bright as the tip of his rifle barrel. It'd only take one shot. She'd be free to cross a continent and an ocean. She could leave her footprints on another mountain and speak to her ancestors in a language he'd heard many times during his own travels but had never taken the time to learn.

He'd been too hell-bent on becoming the best at

walking the narrow path that Jellon preached. He'd thought he'd seen Jellon clearly, but he hadn't.

Never shoot until you see, with clear eyes, what you might kill.

Before him stood a man driven by pride and an endless craving to be admired. He'd been the same. He understood what had pushed him back then—a voice with just enough truth in its lies to stir a man's hunger to never give up the chase.

He chose his words carefully. "You said you saw one of the Bellamy brothers. If he had recognized you, he'd have fled. Down that shaft you dug. Up the other side. Through the stacks of bones you piled. A quick leap across another hole made by you. He'll pause outside, believing he's escaped and needing to catch his breath. He'll wonder if his sister will join him."

"He wouldn't wait for her. He doesn't care about anyone."

"If that's the case, you know what he's doing."

"He's running again," Jellon replied without hesitation.

"Not looking back or bothering to cover his tracks. Certain no one follows. He knows you've given up."

"I haven't," Jellon growled. "But he has. He abandons everyone. Like a yellow-bellied skunk. Like you." Jellon's voice rose to a roar. "You'll all pay for your cowardice."

A gunshot cracked the air. Jellon's bellow morphed into a high-pitched howl.

He fell to his knees, cried out again, and crashed onto his side. He clutched his leg. "You shot me!"

"*Non, croque-mitaine.* He did not." Duval strolled out of the shadows, revolver in one hand and a coil of rope in the other. "He waited too long and left the task to me."

"You ran away!"

"*Non.* Wrong again. I went to retrieve the gear in my pack. My lantern broke in the melee with the bats. I had to find my way in absolute darkness. A time-consuming endeavor, but worth every second." Duval touched his rope to his brow in a salute as his gaze met Lachlan's. "Since I now hold the means to subdue your demon."

Grunting and growling like the bear whose fur he'd taken, Jellon struggled to stand.

"*Non, non, non.*" Duval shook his revolver at Jellon like a scolding finger. "Do not make me put another bullet in you. Stay down. Accept your fate. This is my discovery, not yours. You will be tied up, taken out, and left with the nearest authorities."

"You came back to finish what you couldn't do years ago." Jellon lay on his back, glaring up at Duval. "You plan to take me to a reporter. You still need me to make your name."

"I do not require you for that. This cave is all I need." Duval's nose wrinkled in disgust. He set his coil of rope on his shoulder and waved his hand in front of his face like a fan. "You are nothing more than a smelly lump of fur blocking my road to fame and fortune."

Jellon's bellow echoed off the walls. He kicked Duval in the leg. He kept kicking as the Frenchman fell. His foot struck Duval's revolver. The glint of the barrel arced through the air before vanishing into the darkness.

Jellon rolled onto his hands and one foot. Dragging his injured leg behind him, he crawled and hopped across the stone, scrambling toward the shadows and Duval's revolver.

Élodie grasped Duval's arm and tried to lift him to his feet. "We need to retrieve your gun before Jellon does and starts shooting at us."

"Jellon knows every inch of this cavern. Even outnumbered three to one, he has a better chance of finding that revolver before we do." Despite his words, Lachlan took Duval's other arm and helped her haul the groaning man upright.

"He's used to finding his way in the dark." Élodie's eyes met his. "We need to blind him with light."

"Where are your flares?" Lachlan snagged Duval by his coat collar and swung the man to face him.

Duval's hand was already in his pocket. He pulled out a single stick. "I lost all but one."

"One will do." Élodie thrust her lantern toward him. "Light it."

Even knowing what was coming couldn't prepare Lachlan for how bright the flare would be when standing a stride away. Too late, he raised his hands to shield his eyes from the blazing white. Dazzling dots of reflected light blurred his vision. He blinked hard and fast, striving to gain a clear view of whatever the light might reveal around them.

Jellon crouched on the floor with his robe wrapped tightly over and around him. Duval's revolver rested on the ground between them.

The three of them sprinted forward. At the clatter of their footsteps, Jellon exploded into action. Clutching his robe over his eyes, he blindly swiped his arm in front of him as he limped toward them.

Lachlan's own limp slowed his pace. Duval surged ahead. He reached the revolver first and kicked the gun away from Jellon and back toward them.

Jellon pivoted in a half circle, tracking the scrape of the gun skidding across the stone.

Without a word or a murmur of victory, Élodie scooped up the gun. Only the rasping of their breaths followed.

"You've found it," Jellon said. "No matter. The time has come to use what I found before you came." Jellon let his robe fall from his face. He kept his eyes closed as he reached into a pocket sewn under his buckskin shirt. He drew out a cylindrical stick the same size as Duval's.

"You found one of my flares."

With his eyes still shut, Jellon thrust his stick in the direction of Duval's voice. "Take a closer look. You'll see a gift from another intruder. Didn't the prospector mention he dropped a few tools of his trade during his flight?"

Duval jumped back and held his flare as far away from Jellon as possible. "*Merde,* is that dynamite?"

"I would've lit it long ago, but I lacked a spark. Now you carry a fireball. We must embrace in a glorious conflagration."

"Crawl back into your hellhole, *croque-mitaine.* You will not destroy my triumph." Duval spun around and took off at a full sprint.

With his dynamite in his outstretched hand, Jellon leapt after him. He fell in Duval's wake. The claws on his arm hooked Duval's trouser leg.

Duval toppled as well. With his flare above his head, he rolled and broke free. Still rolling, he hit the wall beside the shaft Jellon had built. He came to a stop without a direct path to flee.

With a cry of victory, Jellon sprang to his feet and, seemingly oblivious to the pain from his gunshot wound, used both legs to charge straight at Duval.

Duval clambered into the hole in a mad rush of lurching light.

Only a few seconds prevented Jellon from catching his quarry. The glow below bathed his face in a ghoulish cast as he reached down after him. "I've got you!"

"*Non!*" A torrent of thumps and grunts followed Duval's plummeting cry. After the briefest of silences, a storm of French curses marked his survival. Duval had the luck of a cat with multiple lives.

Jellon raised his head. A smirk twisted his mouth as he drew his arm from the hole. A sizzling spark raced up the fuse toward the dynamite still clutched in his hand.

Élodie yanked Lachlan in the opposite direction. "Run!"

A giant fist of exploding air slammed his back. He caught hold of Élodie and wrapped his body around her like a shield against whatever came next.

He struck the ground hard. A hailstorm of rock and heat pummeled him like brimstone spewed straight from hell. A wave of dirt descended. He closed his eyes. Gasped for air. Choked on dust. Pressed his face to the rock beneath him and waited for the ringing in his ears to end.

Gentle fingers brushed his cheek. A firm hand shook his shoulder. From far away, Élodie shouted his name.

He opened his eyes and stared into a pair of hazel eyes squinting at him through a gray haze growing darker by the second. Élodie's gaze went to the mangled lantern in her hand. Its flame flickered on the verge of snuffing out.

An eerie moaning came closer. A man staggered out of the dust. He dragged a long, trailing item that scratched the stone like claws.

Lachlan scrambled to locate his Winchester or Élodie's rifle. He found only rocks. He grabbed a stone the size of his fist and raised it toward Jellon.

Élodie's hand on his arm halted him. "He's dying. The explosion hit him full in the chest."

And his face as well.

His mentor was now completely unrecognizable as the legend he'd revered or the beast he'd feared. Jellon sank to his knees. With a sigh of acceptance, he released the bloody breastplate he'd spent years assembling. It had wounded him as much as the dynamite when the blast turned the claws against him.

Jellon used his freed hand to ease himself to the ground. Then he moved no more.

The lantern flame hissed. Its light vanished before Lachlan could turn and see Élodie one last time. An impenetrable darkness stole her from his sight.

It couldn't rob the warmth of her hand on his arm or the resolve in her voice. "The world holds too much light to stay dark forever. We'll find our way."

"I've already found mine. I'm walking out of here

with you." He struggled to stand. Numerous sharp pains kept him down.

Her grip on him tightened. "What hurts the most?"

"My leg." He ran his hand down the limb. Straight. Unbroken. And wet with blood. Cut from his fall or flying shrapnel. He'd need his sight to determine more. He ripped his sleeve from his shirt and tied it tightly around his leg.

"Is it as bad as when we first met?"

"Dragging me to safety this time won't be necessary. I'll hop the entire way on one foot if need be."

"You should lean on me and save your strength for later."

He followed the sound of her voice straight to her lips. He bowed his head and rested his forehead against hers. "Yes."

"Yes, what?"

"I'm saying yes to anything that brings us closer. I always will."

She slung his arm over her shoulder. Her palm slid across his back but stopped abruptly. Her hesitation was as unusual as it was puzzling. They both knew she'd better wrap her arm around him tightly if she wanted to not only get him up but keep him up.

"Show me where I can place my hand."

She was loath to touch the old injury he'd aggravated while dodging Jellon and assisting Duval. He shouldn't have helped the Frenchman. Duval would've fared better if he'd stayed in that first hole. Was he now buried under a mountain of rock? To hope he'd got out the way they'd come was a long shot.

They wouldn't learn Duval's fate sitting here. He needed to get on his feet so they could start moving.

Using his voice, he led Élodie's palm to the least painful spot on his side. Then he heaved himself upward. She provided the additional push required. With their arms around each other, they walked as one.

She adapted her pace to his laborious, limping stride. "We need to find the nearest wall."

He raised his free arm straight out in front of them and searched the dark. "It'll guide us to the light we glimpsed earlier." It'd also take some of his weight from her shoulders.

His fingertips brushed stone. He set his palm against its solidness and they followed the upward incline. For how long, he couldn't guess. Time was elusive in the dark. But each scrape of their footsteps ticked like a clock. It had already been late in the day when they entered the cave. Had darkness descended outside as well?

"Our light had the pink of a setting sun," Élodie said as if pondering the same question.

"The sun may be gone, but the opening its rays touched isn't."

"What if we passed the skylight already?" She halted. "If we did, we might walk forever in the dark."

He leaned against the wall, so she bore less of his weight. "I cannot ask you to carry my weight forever."

"Yes, you can. I know you won't, though." The warmth of her hand found his. She pulled his palm away from the wall and pressed it to her heart instead. "You should know something as well. I'd choose a single day in the dark *with you* over a life-time in the light *without you*. I'm not going anywhere without you."

A sudden dizziness made him slump even harder against the rock. His joy that Élodie might become a permanent part of his life transformed into dread. So much had changed since they'd entered this cave. One inescapable prospect had not.

His weakness still had the power to destroy her.

"You're tired." Her heart pounded under his hand, but her voice remained calm. "We'll rest here and rally our strength for tomorrow. We'll find the light in the morning."

Doubt needled him. Right now he had enough strength to stand with her help. Tomorrow might be a different matter. He had to get Élodie out of here now.

He scanned the darkness. A faint variation turned him as stiff as a hound catching a scent.

"What do you see?" Élodie's question was breathless with anticipation.

"I'm not sure." He didn't blink. "My eyes might be playing tricks on me."

"Show me where to look." She raised their clasped hands and extended their arms together like a pointer.

He couldn't glimpse any part of their bodies, but he saw where he wished to direct her attention. He aimed at a minuscule pinprick of light.

"Starlight!" Her declaration mirrored his hope. "It must mark the bat hole to the sky. You've done it. You've found our way out."

He hugged her close, wanting to bury the treasure of holding her in his arms deep in his heart. That way, whatever happened next, he'd always have this memory. "We found it together."

He kept her close when they pushed away from the wall and shuffled blindly toward the dot of light. His toe bashed something hard. Élodie's arms kept him from falling.

He used his boot to search the ground ahead of them. The uniform smoothness of the lava tube had ended. "Our path is strewn with rocks."

"Take the first step," Élodie urged. "I'll follow."

He set his foot on the nearest rock and levered himself up. He waited for her to join him. Together, they climbed one halting step at a time. They only stopped when the single light became several clustered directly above them.

They stood on rocks that had fallen to form an escape route.

"Can you reach the rim?" Élodie cleaved her body to his again. She steadied him as he found his footing.

With one arm around her, he put his weight on his uninjured leg and stretched his other arm straight up. "I'm a body short."

The perfect body stood beside him. He didn't waste the opportunity. Drawn by blind instinct and a primitive but pure passion, his lips found hers. He kissed her softly, then hard, like he might never kiss her again.

If he never got out of this cavern, he'd take this kiss with him and use its power to rise from the dead. He'd return as a spirit walker to guard Élodie's well-being. His first priority had always been his need to protect her. Now was no different.

"Time to stand on my shoulders," he whispered against her lips.

She ended their kiss but didn't leave the circle of his arms. "I'm not abandoning you."

"Of course you aren't. You're saving me. You're going to get help."

"I won't let you stay down here with Jellon."

"He no longer has the power to hurt me. Even if he returned as the spirit walker we once imagined him to be, he cannot defeat me. Not with the light of your love strengthening me."

Her fingers curled into fists clutching his shirt. She held on tight and pressed her face to his chest. "We leave together or not at all. We're a team."

"If we wish to be a good team, difficult decisions must be made and agreed upon."

"It was easier making decisions alone," she muttered.

"I don't believe that's true."

She heaved a frustrated breath. "Neither do I. But I still choose not to leave you. I won't say anymore."

"Do not deprive me of your voice when I can now picture a future made strong by words."

"I won't accept any future without you."

"If we part, I promise to make our reunion sweet."

A rush of heat flooded her body. "I always suspected you'd possess a talent for cajoling. How do you envision this future strengthened by words?"

"We discuss. We argue. We compromise. When we come to an agreement, we seal it with a handshake." He laid his palm over one of her hands gripping his shirt.

She let go and clasped his hand instead. "I'd prefer a kiss."

"So would I. But first comes the discussion."

Her hand stiffened, then relaxed. "Once I'm out, I'll pull you up."

"You won't be able to reach me."

"I'll hold down a tree branch."

"My weight would pull you back down. We need a rope."

She angled her body in the direction they'd come. "We'll go back and find Alexandre's."

"His rope is under a ton of rock." Hopefully Duval wasn't buried with it. "You'll find what you need in Fort Shelton." She wouldn't be alone. "You go. I wait here."

She pressed close to him again. "I wouldn't be gone long."

"And I'm not going anywhere." He leaned down but stopped with his lips hovering over hers. "Once you're outside, don't look back. The faster you move, the sooner you'll come back to me. Agreed?"

"Agreed." She pressed her lips with his and sealed the agreement with a fiery kiss that promised a volatile future. He wouldn't want it any other way.

When he finally lifted his head, he fixed his gaze on a wall of black. He mustn't waver. He must stand as still as stone. "Climb onto my back and then my shoulders."

She scrambled up nimbly. He gritted his teeth, widened his stance and supported her weight on both legs. He wouldn't let her fall.

"I can't reach it. I'm short an arm's length. I'm

coming down. We tried your way. Now it's time to discuss another."

"Let's try one more time. Agreed?"

Her impatience rumbled above him like a soft growl of thunder. "Agreed."

"Tell me you're reaching for the sky." He slid his hands down her legs to grasp her heels.

"I am. What are you doing?"

"Giving you the arm's length required." With his palms under her feet, he heaved her upward and extended his arms straight above his head.

Her feet left his hands. His gaze immediately shot upward in search of her. The sudden change of focus toppled his balance. He rolled quickly onto his back so he could see where she'd gone.

He saw only an empty hole, a portal between life and death, between earth and the heavens. Élodie had vanished like a dream too good to be true.

When he'd hauled fugitives to jail, he'd brought them to a similar doorway. He'd chosen never to cross with them. He'd waited for the guards to come and complete that final step. He'd steered clear of the inescapable loneliness the doomed men faced inside.

He now faced his.

He'd been driven by the hunt, the need to move, to always keep advancing. Inside this cave, he'd gone further than he ever hoped he could. He'd done his best to save Élodie from his past and from hers.

He'd succeeded. Her bravery had resurrected his. But peace remained elusive.

Élodie's light was gone. Without her, he'd be forever condemned to loneliness.

He'd spend every future breath wishing for a glimpse of her smile, the warmth of her hand, the sweetness of her kiss. That was his sentence. He willingly accepted it. He closed his eyes and focused on her memory. In his mind, he held her in his arms. It had to be a dream because the warmth of her spirit embraced him as well.

Whatever it was—whatever *she* was, she was enough for him.

He'd wait an eternity for her return.

CHAPTER 8

Élodie's beloved mountain's usually reviving breeze turned her shivers to shudders as she lay on its unforgiving rock and peered into its belly. The cavern below gaped in a bottomless black pit. No sight or sound of Lachlan. Each second she'd spent outside the warmth of his embrace overwhelmed her with a loneliness that stretched like an eternity.

"Lachlan Bravery! Tell me you're still there. Speak to me. I need your voice."

"I'm here." The deep resonance of his reply filled the void and snuffed out her fears. Lachlan was a survivor. Even the most brutal and insane darkness couldn't defeat him. He was a legend in life and in her heart.

"But why are you here? What happened to our agreement?"

The apprehension in his question prompted her swift answer. "It changed when I found Monsieur Duval a few minutes after I left you. Or rather, he and I found each other as he came up the mountain and I went down."

"Happy to hear he survived the explosion. Why wasn't he heading back to the fort?"

She glanced at Alexandre, suddenly wondering the same.

Outlined in muted starlight, he sat beside her with his head on his arms and his arms on his knees. He wheezed and coughed, struggling to catch his breath after not only their recent climb but the miraculous feat of escaping the explosion. His beautiful frock coat hung in tatters down his back. Dust and shards of stone shrouded him like a second skin.

When she pushed her hair back from her face, she discovered the blast had covered her as well.

Alexandre shrugged but didn't lift his head. "I remembered you proclaiming an object *extraordinaire* existed up here. I decided to have a view."

"You decided you had to help us." She leapt up and hugged him, then rushed back to call down to Lachlan. "Do you now recognize how fabulous Alexandre is? He not only held onto our friendship, he held onto his rope! One end is now tied to a tree and the other will soon be in your hands." She threw the rope into the darkness and prayed it was long enough.

"Got it."

Her heart swelled with joy, then pinched with worry as the cord went taut under Lachlan's weight. If he lost his grip and fell—

"Hold on tight. We'll pull you up." Taking a seat close to the hole, she braced her feet on the rock and pulled hard on the line.

"Can he not climb out on his own? I could use some rest. I barely survived an explosion." Alexandre's dour tone couldn't diminish her budding excitement that Lachlan would soon be in her arms again.

"All three of us survived an explosion. We did it together. Now get behind me and help me pull."

Alexandre complied, and together they heaved.

"*Mon Dieu,*" he grumbled. "He is as heavy as a brick house."

The top of Lachlan's head appeared. Covered in dust and blown wild by the blast, his hair looked identical to Alexandre's. His deep, gravelly voice remained unchanged and unique to him. "I can't be heavier than you were, Duval, when we hauled you out of your hole."

An undertone of laughter in his voice made her grin and gave her the strength to pull even harder.

Lachlan's hands moved in the silvery light as he climbed up the rope. He wasn't hanging still and waiting for them to pull him up. With each movement, he emitted a low grunt or a rumbling growl. He wasn't hiding his pain now.

She pulled harder. "You don't have to climb anymore. We've almost got you out."

Peering over the rock, Lachlan's eyes glinted like blue stars against a face as dusty and gray as his hair. "Is that fabulous friend you praised still bellyaching about my weight or is he pulling with you?" When his gaze found her, a flash of white revealed his smile and his happiness to see her. "My beautiful dust-covered angel, I observe no one else but you saving me again."

The tension on the cord behind her told her Alexandre was still there.

His voice shot over her shoulder, tight and terse and most likely from between gritted teeth. "On the count of three, I will pull one last time and show you who is here and how hard they have been pulling. *Un. Deux. Trois!*"

She heaved with all her might. Alexandre must have as well because Lachlan flew up and out and landed on top of her. His weight knocked the air from her lungs. That didn't stop her from wrapping her arms around him and hugging him even closer.

Muttering a curse and an apology, he rolled onto his side with his arms around her as well.

Air flowed into her lungs. So did the urge to shout with joy. The dust covering her and Lachlan reduced her elation to a fit of coughing. "No doubt about it," she wheezed, then managed a hoarse chuckle. "You're heavy."

"Good Lord." Lachlan's hands shot up to cradle her face and raise her gaze to his. "I've finally hurt you. How badly are you injured?"

"I'm not wounded."

"But you're in pain."

"My pain is manageable." She used her best soothing tone, willing him to trust the words. "How's yours?"

A devilish spark lit his eyes as he studied her. "You've tuckered me out. It'd be best if I rested in your arms the entire night before I attempted to get up."

"We remain in harmony." She snuggled closer and pressed her ear to his chest so she could listen to his heart beating, strong and fast and hopefully free from the voice that had hounded him.

Alexandre huffed out a breath and flopped down on the ground beside them. "My pains are manageable as well. Thank you for asking."

A chuckle rumbled in Lachlan's chest.

"This is no laughing matter," Alexandre protested. "My grand discovery has been reduced to rubble."

"Jellon's rock pile and shaft took the brunt of the explosion." The memory of its violence made her shiver.

"It contained it as well." Lachlan's hands rubbed her back and warmed her. "With the dust cloud and the lantern on its final glimmer, I cannot be certain, but I think the rest of your lava tube survived."

"*Alléluia!*" Alexandre bounded up, and his feet drummed the ground in a jig. His puffing slowed his steps but couldn't mute the jubilation in his voice. "An astronomical stroke of luck. Praise the heavens. A thousand thanks."

Lachlan stiffened. "Not everyone was so lucky."

"He's finally at rest," she whispered. "Let his memory go with him."

Alexandre's footfalls halted. "The man in the cavern is dead? You called him by name. You knew him well."

"The man I knew died a long time ago."

Alexandre reclaimed his seat near them. "Today your friend took his final step in this world. Tonight he strides across a new land. When my society continues this cave's exploration, I will ask the expedition leader to give him a proper burial—free of that abyss but still on this mountain."

Lachlan cleared his throat gruffly. "A hunter couldn't ask for a better place to sleep."

Alexandre's next words drifted up and away as if he contemplated the sky. "The atmosphere is peaceful here. The sky soars, and the stars are infinite. They cover everything."

A thousand pinpricks of silver dotted the blanket

of indigo high above them. Its glory outshone both the rising moon and the humbler lights that glowed in the branches below the star-studded sky.

Her lips parted in a gasp. "These are the lights I glimpse from below. They guided us to safety after the sun sank." Tears blurred her eyes and made her voice husky. *"Votre lumière est toujours avec moi. Merci, Papa et Maman.* Thank you for always showing the way."

"I have never observed lights such as these," Alexandre remarked. "Do you explain them by science or magic?"

"They may be a combination of both." Lachlan's lips brushed her hair.

Élodie sighed deeply as she relaxed in the warmth of his love and contemplated the earth's many marvels. "Some call them glowworms. Others say fireflies."

"They're one of a mountain's tiniest and most resilient creatures." Lachlan kissed the top of her head as he pulled her even closer. "They've lit our past. They will do the same for our future."

"A comforting notion, but too fantastical for my world. No matter. My path is set." Alexandre climbed to his feet and brushed off his clothes. "I must return to Fort Shelton and face my team."

"Will you head east after that?" Lachlan asked.

"Oui, bien sûr. And you shall stay here with the lovely Mademoiselle Rousseau."

"I still wish to visit France one day," Élodie said with determination.

"And you will," Alexandre replied. "But first, you must explore what lies between here and there."

"Thank you. Sincerely. Your help is appreciated more than you can imagine." Lachlan's arms tightened around her, then relaxed as he released a sigh that sounded resigned but also at ease. "Can we help you find your way back to Fort Shelton, Mr. Duval?"

"*Mr.* Duval?" Alexandre echoed in an incredulous tone. He gave a loud whoop. "After the long and arduous day we have shared, you should know me well enough to call me Alex."

"If that's the case," Lachlan replied, "you know what to call me."

Alexandre grabbed them both by the arm. Standing above them, he leaned closer and grinned. "*Mes amis*, you must savor this moment. I shall never be this agreeable again. Now I will leave you two lovebirds alone and stroll down to Fort Shelton guided by the many lights around us."

A frown pinched her brow. "Sounds like a lonely walk. If you wait, we could accompany you when the sun rises."

"*Non,* my impatience grows and besides I will never be alone." He pulled his journal from his coat pocket and raised it above his head like a torch. "Not as long as I have the records of my travels and the ability to keep adding to them." He winked at her. "I carry detailed descriptions of every path I have traversed, including the one from here to Fort Shelton along which you guided not only my fine self but also"—he tilted his head toward Lachlan— "someone else's extremely lucky donkey's ass."

Lachlan's unbound laughter made them join in.

"What are we laughing about?" Alexandre asked.

"The increasing beauty of words," Lachlan replied. "I would've called myself a jackass instead of donkey's ass."

"As you wish." Alexandre whistled a cheerful tune as he walked away. He only paused long enough to call back, "Farewell, Monsieur Jackass and Mademoiselle Élodie."

In the silence that followed, she snuggled closer to Lachlan. Walking down her mountain under a canopy of lights in the sky and trees would be magnificent, but holding Lachlan was a thousand times better. "We are now a team of two."

"With you by my side, I'll gladly give up hunting people and start guiding them."

"Our future doesn't have to narrow to one path. To deprive the world of a great tracker would be a crime. Some lost loved ones may never be found, but that doesn't mean we should stop looking."

"Finding a happy face at the end of a search would be a pleasant change. But my greatest challenges may always come from within." His voice went hoarse with apprehension. "What if, even with Jellon finally at rest, my voice returns?"

Her hand rose to comfort him. Without hesitation, he pressed his cheek to her palm, but his jaw remained hard and his teeth stayed clenched.

"We will greet every voice promptly. Like wild creatures, we must face them and stand firm. Together we will calm your inner demons." Or at least distract them. She strove for a way to do that now. "Our partnership could use a name."

The tension in his jaw eased. "Team Bravery?" he suggested in a wry but wistful tone.

She caressed his scars with her fingertips. "Or simply the Braveries."

"Once again, you are the wisest of guides." He cleared his throat gruffly, then continued in a rush, "Will you marry me? I promise to do everything I can to make you happy."

"You've already done that. No matter how dark or bright. The only light I need shines in you." She leaned back so she could search his eyes. She was well rewarded.

His love and fidelity blazed brighter than ever as he watched her. He didn't blink as he asked, "Can you see that I still want to kiss you?"

"I see a today and many tomorrows filled with numerous kisses." A willing smile curved her lips. "I have no choice. Even if I did, I wouldn't choose differently. You are my bravery, my strength, and my destiny."

He nodded solemnly. "As you are mine."

"We remain in harmony."

"Time to make our agreement official." His gaze locked on her mouth hungrily. "I'm waiting to hear you say you'll marry me."

"I will. You're my only choice, Lachlan Bravery. You always have been and always will be." She pressed her lips to his and sealed their future with a kiss.

~

Thanks for reading Élodie & Lachlan's story!

Élodie made her first appearance as the fearless six-year-old Yellow Feather when she joined Eagle Feather and Faith Featherby's journey in *Following Faith*. I'm very happy she kept talking to me and showed me the path to her own happily-ever-after. I couldn't wait for her and Lachlan to get into and then out of that cave.

Keep turning the page to see how writing a review can make an author's day, or to read my inspiration for writing *Choosing Bravery,* or to read excerpts from...

- *The Calling Birds* (my first Noelle Christmas book)
- *Between Love & Lies* (book 1 in my *Gambling Hearts* series)
- *Following Faith*

Wishing you happy reading,
Jacqui

DEAR READER

I hope you enjoyed Élodie & Lachlan's adventure in the Cascade Mountains.

If you did, please consider posting a review online or email it to me at Jacqui@JacquiNelson.com

Every single review helps. No matter how long or short, they are a heartfelt gift that is sincerely appreciated. Hearing from readers makes my day and keeps me motivated to write my next book. Looking forward to hearing from you!

You can review *Choosing Bravery* on Amazon, Goodreads, or BookBub. Or even all three.

AMAZON
amazon.com/author/jacquinelson

GOODREADS
goodreads.com/jacquinelson

BOOKBUB
bookbub.com/authors/jacqui-nelson

STORY INSPIRATION & NOTES

While writing *Following Faith* and watching six-year-old Élodie Rousseau become such a fundamental part (even while mostly off screen), I knew my next story had to be her grown-up adventure. I also knew she needed a larger-than-life man to match her big personality.

A decade or more before, I'd met someone with the surname Bravery and tucked it away for future use. The right story hero never appeared to claim the name. After writing *Following Faith* and watching *The Revenant,* I knew Élodie's match would be a legendary, almost mythical mountain man. A man who'd been brought low by a bear, but could be lifted high by Élodie and her mountain home. A man named Bravery.

When my research led me to Oregon's Cascade Volcanic Arc, Newberry Volcano, and lava tubes, I knew the majority of their story would be underground—a challenging place to describe. When travel isn't an option, a writer relies on pictures. I created a Pinterest board to help me visualize the story. For links to *Choosing Bravery's* picture board and boards created for my other stories, visit my website JacquiNelson.com

~ Jacqui

THE CALLING BIRDS

~

A wanted woman's flight, a man in pursuit of honesty, not stolen gold...and only nine days left to save the town.

Many years have passed since Bernadette Bellamy fled the Cariboo Gold Rush and her reputation as the sister of a French-Canadian gang of thieves. Armed with only an honest talent for sewing and a willingness to lead a solitary life on the run, she stays one step ahead of everyone seeking her brothers' last—and now lost—heist. Until a craving to settle down makes her reinvent herself as Birdie Bell, a dress shop owner. The arrival of an old foe combined with her desire to hold onto her treasure trove of fabrics has Birdie joining a wagonload of brides bound for a remote town.

After losing his leg in the War Between the States and his wife in the years following, Jack Peregrine buries his pain under a mountain-high pile of work. He only agrees to sign up for a mail-order bride to save the town of Noelle, keep his freighting business, and care for his absentminded grandfather. But Jack's request for a sturdy bride who won't crumble under his burdens brings him a woman as tiny as she is troubled.

Can two mismatched people band together to become the perfect match?

~

THE CALLING BIRDS ~ EXCERPT

Noelle, Colorado
December 24, 1876

A crowd of women filled *La Maison's* front hall. One of them was Jack's bride, Birdie Bell. A hard-working woman who'd started her own dressmaking business in Denver. A mature woman of thirty. A strong woman who wouldn't break under life's hardships.

Maybe his luck would change today. With time Miss Bell might come to respect or maybe even enjoy his company. He needed this marriage to last.

He should've looked for his grandfather first, but he couldn't stop his gaze from scanning the women in search of his bride. Even wild-swept from the storm and huddled together shivering from the cold, the women were a fine-looking bunch. How had Mrs. Walters managed that?

A raven-haired, pale-skinned woman standing slightly apart from the rest snared his attention. Her beauty would've been enough to hold any man spell-bound, but her tiny size turned him rigid with concern. A woman so small wouldn't last long in a town like Noelle.

His worry turned to anger. Whoever had asked her to come here should be horsewhipped!

A faint smile curved her mouth as if she was amused by the prospect of being housed in a location as scandalous as La Maison. He must be dreaming. She shouldn't be here and she couldn't be amused.

She surveyed the room, studying everything and everyone—until she saw him. Then she stared at him the way he felt he must be staring at her, as if mesmerized.

"I've come for a bride," a voice proclaimed loudly, a familiar voice that made him cringe. "Which one of you is the future Mrs. Peregrine?"

The woman spun to face the speaker—his Grandpa Gus.

A wave of gasps and tittering laughter swept through the crowd. Several of the women glanced at the tiny woman who'd captivated him. She was now staring at Gus with wide eyes.

Her gaze darted to him. When she caught him still staring at her, her expression turned blank and devoid of emotion. She straightened her shoulders, strode straight up to Gus, and said in a lyrical voice with a seductively foreign accent, "I am the bride you seek, Mr. Peregrine. My name is Birdie Bell."

A surge of euphoria followed quickly by alarm made him stagger and lean heavily against the nearest wall. This tiny Frenchwoman couldn't be Miss Bell. He'd asked for a strong woman. This one wouldn't be able to hold up under his workload, the rough town, or the surrounding wilderness. She'd abandon Noelle and him.

Could he blame her if she did?

If she didn't, she might die here.

"No!" His voice shot out louder than Gus' a moment ago.

Complete silence descended around him. The chance to make a good impression was long gone. Everyone in the front hall stared at him, including his tiny bride.

He limped toward her.

Her gaze dropped to his leg, and her lips parted on a gasp. When their eyes met again, she smiled. He'd told her in his letter that he'd lost a leg in the war. She'd guessed who he was.

Did the prospect of marrying him please her, or was she merely relieved she wouldn't be marrying a man forty years older than her?

He realized he'd written that Peregrines' Post and Freight was a family run business, but he'd been remiss in not describing the members of his family.

"Sorry for being late. I'm Jack Peregrine and this

is my grandfather, Gus Peregrine. Will you—" He'd been about to ask if she'd come home with him and stay in his brother Max's empty room. It'd be better than residing in a whorehouse, but it probably wouldn't be appropriate for them to live together before they were married.

He could ask her to say her vows with him right now and then—

What if she said no? What if she said yes?

Her smile faded to a shadow of its former brilliance. She raised her chin and studied him with eyes dark as blue twilight and glittering with questions. She'd soon see that they weren't the right match. But he needed a wife.

He needed to reassess his plans.

"I'll call on you tomorrow, Miss Bell. I must take my grandfather home." He grabbed Gus by the elbow and pulled him away.

His bride's gaze stayed on him until he crossed *La Maison's* threshold and shut the door behind him.

To read more about *The Calling Birds*, visit
JacquiNelson.com

Keep reading for another excerpt...

BETWEEN LOVE & LIES
Gambling Hearts Series - Book 1

Sadie Sullivan lost everything when a herd of longhorn cattle bound for Dodge City trampled and destroyed her farm. Now she works in Dodge—one of the most wicked and lawless towns in the West—at the Northern Star Saloon. But her survival in this new world of sin and violence depends on maintaining a secret so deadly it could end her life before the town of Dodge can.

The one man capable of unraveling all of Sadie's secrets is Noah Ballantyne, the Texan rancher whose herd destroyed her home. Back in town and taking up the role of deputy alongside legendary lawman Bat Masterson, Noah vows he won't leave until he's made things right. But with the saloon's madam unwilling to release Sadie and a rich cattle baron wanting her as well, the odds aren't in favor of finding love...or leaving town alive.

~

CHAPTER 1

South of Dodge City, Kansas
May 1, 1876

They were destroying everything: the tiny apple tree she'd sheltered in the wagon during the long, sweltering journey from Virginia; the fence she'd devoted weeks to repairing over the winter with scraps of deadwood; the vegetable garden she'd sown during the first whisper of spring and painstakingly coaxed to life every heartbeat since.

All trampled, devoured, gone.

Sadie glared at the beasts, eyes burning with tears of hopeless rage. Graceless creatures, they wielded heavy horns that stretched out of their skulls like spears. Texas longhorns. The Devil's helpers.

In the middle of them rode Lucifer himself, sent straight up from hell to torment her and tear away everything she'd slaved to build.

She tracked the long-legged, well-built rider as he steered his horse through the milling animals, angling toward her and her father—and their sod house. Dismay tightened her throat, left her bereft of air and hope. Even that stalwart structure was in danger of being leveled by the heaving mass in the care of the man coming ever closer.

The intruder, similar to all the other Texas drovers, was covered in a layer of trail dust so thick it hung on him like a second skin. But it was one of the only things he and the other men had in common. While the rest hollered and cracked whips over the backs of the beasts in their charge—trying to persuade them to return to the trail—this man urged his charcoal-colored mount through the river of hide and horn, making a beeline for her.

His silence, along with his ability to guide his horse with remarkably little effort, infuriated her. As the distance between them shortened, unease crept up her spine.

His gaze was unwavering, never leaving her.

She tightened her grip on the ancient shotgun clutched at her side, and concentrated on her anger and frustration, transferring them from the long-horns to settle solely on him. She did not want him to come any closer.

Yanking the shotgun up to her shoulder, she took aim.

The cowboy straightened in his saddle but otherwise did not acknowledge her hostile action. Nor did he slacken his pace; if anything, he bore down on her even faster.

Damn him to hell. Her finger tightened on the trigger.

Something slammed down on her shotgun, pitching the rusted barrel earthward. The buckshot tore a savage gouge out of the clay in front of her and kicked up a cloud of dust. The blast forced her to stumble back.

Her father's red face inserted itself between her and the cowboy. With a curse, he jerked the weapon from her grasp.

As she stood gawking at him, the cattle, spooked by the shotgun blast, bolted—fast and in every direction. Her father sprinted toward their lone plow horse, scrambled onto its back and galloped away from the melee and her.

She shouldn't have expected anything different. Still, the hurt came. Sharp and deep. Once again he'd thought only of himself. He'd abandoned her in the center of the herd, alone and defenseless.

I'm going to be trampled. I'm going to die.

To read more about *Between Love & Lies*, visit JacquiNelson.com

Keep reading for another excerpt...

FOLLOWING FAITH
Lonesome Hearts Series

*Can a single day together on horseback
change your life forever?*

Labeled a harlot and expelled from a remote logging
camp and her work teaching children, Faith
Featherby embarks on a journey to return a stolen
spirit horse to the little girl whose photograph was
hidden in the horse's riding blanket.
Orphaned young and stifled by a lifelong shyness,
Faith has only her education as a schoolmistress and
her memories of her mother's stories. She's not an
experienced rider, but a Medicine Hat horse—
alleged to have the sacred power to protect its rider
—might be her best hope for surviving the
wilderness... until an Osage warrior rides out of the
mist.
Scarred by a brutal past, the warrior challenges Faith
to follow a new path where belief in yourself and
your partner, be they horse or man, can lead to a
triumph of the heart.

Follow a path. Find a partner. Fight for a future together.

∼

CHAPTER 1

Oregon Territory - Autumn 1852

"You're relieved from your duties, Miss Featherby."
Mr. Hammond tucked his bearded chin under his
sagging collar, seeking respite from the squalls that
tested Timber Creek's logging camp more days than
not during Faith Featherby's three years teaching in
the wilderness.

Although she habitually shied away from
confrontations, this wasn't one she could accept
mutely. "For how long? The children need me."

Hovering at the foot of the schoolhouse steps,
Hammond's usually kind eyes remained downcast as
he stared at Faith—or rather her feet, which were
frozen in her bewilderment to the threshold of a
structure that doubled as her lodgings.

"Your presence as Timber Creek's schoolmistress
is no longer desirable," Hammond replied in a staccato voice, as if reciting from a script. Under
eyebrows thick as wooly caterpillars, his eyes darted
left then right, toward Mrs. Cain and Mrs. Crisp,
who flanked him. "The school committee has voted.
You're to leave immediately 'n never return."

An avalanche of fear hit Faith. She clutched the
doorframe of the one-room shanty she'd transformed into a safe haven for her students and
herself. Becoming a teacher had been her ticket out

of the orphanage she'd grown up in. A ticket she'd hoped would lead to a better future.

"I've nowhere to go."

Mrs. Crisp's arctic-blue gaze chilled her to the bone. "You'll find room in a bawdy house."

"Jezebel," Mrs. Cain hissed under her breath.

"Whore of Babylon," Mrs. Crisp added, lightning quick.

A gasp broke from Faith's lips before she could swallow it along with her hurt. From day one, the two women had mistaken her shyness for conceit and never uttered a kind word to her, or about her. But until today, they'd never gone so far as to slander her character.

Hammond raised his palms in a placating manner, but his gaze dipped even lower, locking on his own feet. "Ladies, please. Ain't no need for name callin'."

Mrs. Crisp sniffed in disdain. "She brought this on herself."

"What do you mean?" Faith slumped against the doorway and struggled to speak over her rising panic. "I've done nothing wrong."

Mrs. Cain's spindly body snapped straight as a pencil while her voice climbed high enough to make even Hammond flinch. "You consider relations outside marriage *nothing*?"

"Who said—?" An appalling notion pierced Faith.

Last week Dan Doolan had been furious when she rejected his overtures of *relations outside marriage*, which he'd proclaimed was her only prospect considering her advancing spinsterhood and lack of social graces. He'd preyed on her weaknesses. She could very well end up in a bawdy house —unable to elude men like Doolan—if she lost this job. She had few savings and no family or friends.

She forced herself to stand tall. "I have never participated in relations of those types."

Hammond's eyebrows bunched together as he frowned at the cut line where the woodsmen, including Doolan, labored unseen but still heard. Their constant chopping and cussing filled the air from sunup to sundown.

"You're sayin' Doolan is lyin'?"

If she did not, she'd be branded a harlot. If she did, Doolan would soon be harassing her for slandering *his* name. "He's... not telling the truth." She cringed at the halting quaver in her voice.

Even though Mrs. Crisp stood below Faith, the woman managed to stare down her nose at her. "Mr. Doolan is a long upstanding member of this community."

"I've lived here as long as he has," Faith protested.

Mrs. Cain crossed her arms. "We know him. We do not know you."

Dan Doolan made himself *known* by intruding into people's lives.

Before Faith could round up the gumption to say so, Mrs. Crisp said, "Pegged her for a sinner from the start."

Mrs. Cain gave a curt nod. "Always suspected she was hiding something."

Faith's crippling shyness had prevented her from connecting with anyone in the camp, except for the children she taught. Children had curious minds. Adults often had theirs locked tight. But Mrs. Cain and Mrs. Crisp were right to sense Faith was hiding something. It just wasn't what they currently believed.

"You'd cast me into the wilderness with the"— she gestured to the circle of trees, the lifeblood of this community, and the unknown beyond—"with the wolves?"

"You'll fit right in with them," Mrs. Crisp replied. "And the savages, too. Only you would adopt a crow-bait Indian nag and squander your time nursing it back to health."

"The mare deserved a second chance." The sweet-tempered pinto had been ridden until winded and lame, and then discarded to limp into the camp seeking refuge. "Don't we all?"

Mrs. Cain's exaggerated scoff made her rock like a soaring Ponderosa Pine ready to come crashing down. "Not when our children are involved. Only a dullard such as you would suggest such a thing."

"Always questioned her intelligence."

"Probably lied about her credentials."

"We'll file a complaint so no one ever employs her again."

Mrs. Cain and Crisp's swift exchange left Faith's head spinning.

"No, we won't!" Hammond's voice rose along with his gaze until he finally looked Faith in the eye.

Hope flared in her heart and sprang forth in a grateful smile. He wouldn't let them oust her from her home and livelihood. He'd help her.

He blinked as if dumbfounded, and more than a little bedazzled, by her smile. Hanging onto the suspenders bordering his heart, he burrowed his chin back under his collar. "Miss Featherby, I'm sorry, but the school committee's minds are set." He spun away from Faith and her condemners. Once his feet started moving, he gained speed and didn't stop. "You should get goin' before you make matters worse," he called over his shoulder. "God keep you safe on your journey."

CHAPTER 2

With Timber Creek behind her and the sun struggling to break through the morning mist ahead, Faith stared at the fork in the road. Sitting on Spirit, the mare she'd nursed from footsore to sprightly, she faced the first decision on her journey: take the main road or turn onto the narrow trail that led to Bird's Eye Pass.

Faith stroked Spirit's snowy mane, hoping to draw strength from the mare. Spirit would keep her safe as much as God would.

Even though Mrs. Cain and Mrs. Crisp ridiculed her for helping the mare, she'd never regret that decision. She slid the daguerreotype from the pocket that appeared custom-made for it in the simple riding blanket that served as Spirit's saddle. The photograph showed the mare wearing the same blanket while being ridden by a small blonde girl of maybe six or seven.

She flipped over the photograph and, for the hundredth time, contemplated the printer's stamp, *Little Haven News—Print, Post, Daguerreotypes*, and the carefully written words, *Yellow Feather & Spirit, 1852*.

The photograph had been taken this year. Surely that was a sign as much as Spirit's unique markings. Here lay Faith's future. She'd always gained strength from helping others. Today would be no different.

She would ride Spirit to Little Haven and return the mare to the girl named Yellow Feather. A girl who—judging by how lovingly she smiled at Spirit —must surely be missing her.

But when Faith assessed the two paths ahead,

her unease returned. Before finding Spirit, she'd seldom ridden. A boat and wagon had delivered her from the teacher's academy to Timber Creek. She eyed the puny sack slung over Spirit's shoulders. She'd stuffed it with her meager belongings and enough food for a week if rationed. She was ill-prepared for the journey ahead, not to mention the decisions she must make alone.

~

To read more about *Following Faith*, visit JacquiNelson.com

WANT A FREE E-BOOK?

Deadwood, Dakota Territory 1876...
*In a gold rush storm, can an unlikely pair rescue each
other?*
Raven wants to save one person. Charlie wants to
save the world. Their warring nations thrust them
together but duty pulled them apart—until their
paths crossed again in Deadwood for a fight for love.

EXCERPT
RESCUING RAVEN - CHAPTER 1

Fighting a growing impatience fueled by rage,
Charlie Jennings drew his revolver and urged his
horse through the trees flanking the Deadwood
Trail. Below him, an Appaloosa with the strikingly
similar color of his own horse—white covered from
head to hock in chestnut spots—was rein-tied to the
back of a buckboard. If the horse hadn't caught his
attention, he might not have given the transport a
second look.

He might not have seen her.

The wagon rattled forward carrying one silent and seven grumbling passengers. When a bend in the trail cast the sun in the eyes of the guards, one riding behind and the other in front, he charged his spotted mare down onto the road.

Everyone in the wagon, except for the cowering raven-haired woman, screamed. The driver jerked on the lines. The horses skidded to a halt. The guards scrambled for their weapons.

The click of his revolver being cocked made them all freeze.

The silence that followed was as heated as the summer sun on his back. The guards glared at him through squinted eyes. He kept his focus on them as well—lined up in a neat row down the barrel of his Colt Peacemaker.

"Jennings," growled the closest man, who went by the name Big Bill. "You shouldn't be here."

"Yeah," hollered Bill's partner, a stranger who resembled a beanpole.

Frontier trails and towns had a way of attracting similarly named men, including the Charlies like him. They also had a fondness for embellishment. The deck was stacked in favor of the rear guard being called Skinny Sam or Loudmouth Pete.

"We heard you were guidin' a miner 'n his four kids, the ones who lost their ma, away from Deadwood." At least Skinny hadn't heard, and used, the double-barreled moniker Charlie had been saddled with since arriving in the Black Hills.

"But you," he shot back, "didn't hear that my job finished ahead of schedule."

"Well," Bill said on a long breath, "ain't that a spot of bad luck."

"Not for one of your passengers." He didn't look her way. He'd already seen enough: a ragtag assortment of women, one hunched with her dark head over her wrists tied to the wagon.

To read the rest of *Rescuing Raven*, visit my website JacquiNelson.com and sign up for my newsletter.

Rescuing Raven - Deadwood, 1876, a FREE read for

my newsletter subscribers

∽

GAMBLING HEART SERIES

Between Love & Lies - Book 1, Dodge City, 1877

Between Home & Heartbreak - Book 2, Texas, 1879

∽

STEAM! ROMANCE AND RAILS

Adella's Enemy - Kansas, 1870

∽

To learn more about my books, visit my website

JacquiNelson.com

PRAISE FOR THE GAMBLING HEARTS SERIES...

Between Love & Lies - **Book 1**
"I loved the twists and turns this book takes. If you want a top-shelf historical western romance, you won't go wrong with this." ~ Linda Broday (New York Times & USA Today bestselling author)

"I couldn't read it fast enough and I didn't want it to end either." ~ Bob

"The chemistry in this book sizzles from the very first pages. The characters come to life with vibrant color and intensity." ~ Heather C.

"Held me in its grasp and wouldn't let me go until the oh-so-satisfying conclusion." ~ Diane B.

Between Home & Heartbreak - **Book 2**
"A western romance, thrill ride, filled with twists and turns in every chapter!" ~ A.P.Reader

"A fun, yet nail biting story." ~ Christine W.

"Open the book and get swept away!" ~ Little Piggy's

"Kept my attention until the end! I just loved her heroine Eldorado Jane" ~ Nicole L.

ABOUT THE AUTHOR

Fall in love with a new Old West... where the men are steadfast and the women are adventurous. You'll find Wild West scouts, spies, cardsharps, wilderness guides, and trick-riding superstars in my stories. Those are my heroines. Wait till you meet my heroes!

My love for historical romance adventures with grit and passion came from watching Western movies while growing up on a cattle farm in northern Canada. I've been nominated for over 20 awards and won the RWA® Golden Heart® & the Laramie® — but my best reward is hearing from readers who have enjoyed my stories.

Email me at Jacqui@JacquiNelson.com

For updates on giveaways, special events, and more, join my newsletter at JacquiNelson.com

amazon.com/Jacqui-Nelson/e/B00EE6GE88

goodreads.com/JacquiNelson

bookbub.com/authors/jacqui-nelson

facebook.com/JacquiNelsonAuthor

instagram.com/jacquinelsonauthor

pinterest.com/JacquiAuthor

x.com/Jacqui_Nelson

youtube.com/@jacquinelsonauthor

tiktok.com/@jacquinelsonauthor